DEAD LITTLE MEAN GIRL

DEAD LITTLE MEAN GIRL
HARLEQUIN® TEEN
EVA DARROWS

ISBN-13: 978-0-373-21241-5

Dead Little Mean Girl

This edition published by arrangement with Harlequin Books S.A.

For questions and comments about the quality of this book, please contact us at CustomerService@Harlequin.com.

HARLEQUIN® TEEN
TM www.HarlequinTEEN.com

Printed in U.S.A.

For Becky, who always makes me smile.

CHAPTER ONE

QUINN LITTLETON WAS FOUND FACEDOWN IN MY garage at nine in the morning on a Monday, her corpse dressed up like Malibu Barbie. Her boobs were crammed into a homemade coconut-shell bra that tied off behind her back with pink ribbons. She wore a hula-style grass skirt she'd trimmed so short it barely covered anything, and thanks to her unflattering final position of facedown, rump pointed at the garage doors, the first thing anyone saw of her corpse was a sliver of thong bisecting perfect butt cheeks.

Quinn Littleton was dead.

And it was sorta my fault.

Did I mention she's my sister?

I probably should have explained that with the whole "dead in my garage" thing. Hot, popular girls don't just die there like it's some kind of suburban elephant graveyard. Quinn is—was—related to me. Sort of. She wasn't my birth sister but she was for all intents and purposes my stepsister. The only reason she wasn't my *actual* stepsister is our moms hadn't married yet. So Quinn and I lived together, had rooms next to one another and were forced to endure holidays together all without an actual and factual sisterly bond.

I wouldn't have wanted one, given the choice. We didn't jell.

Quinn was a mean girl. We're not talking "mouthy" or "occasionally moody" or "sharp around the edges." We're talking "full-throttle mega-mean girl with acid spit and laser eyes." That's awful to say about the recently departed, but you had to see her in action to understand. If she didn't like you, she took insidious glee in decimating you until you were a twitching pile of pudding beneath her stilettos. Worse? She got away with it. People allowed a lava-spewing horror show to rule the school because she was hot and popular.

High school is gross.

It didn't help that I'm one of those nerdy girls—brainy, glasses, I wear jeans every day and my morning beauty regime consists of washing my face, brushing my teeth and sticking my hair into a ponytail. It was mortifying for Princess Pedicure, who got up a full hour and a half before we left for school to make sure she had time to set her curlers, apply her makeup and match her underwear to her miniskirts.

There's nothing wrong with investing in your appearance. There is, however, something wrong with telling everyone they're disgusting because they don't go on the latest kale-and-prune-juice diet to be "Africa skinny." That's a direct quote, by the way. Africa skinny.

Quinn's worldview was severely limited.

* * *

Quinn and I met a year after our moms started hanging out. We had no idea that they were getting it on behind closed doors, but they hadn't advertised it, either. They were two quasi-recent divorcées who had joined a women's support group and found one another. It was martinis on Fridays, late-night conversation and a lot of texting. Which became a lot of shopping trips and dinner dates. And weekend day trips. And then full weekend getaways to Cape Cod and weeks in Maine.

Nine months later, my mother sat me down in the kitchen to inform me that she was dating Karen Littleton, who was a lawyer and "a wonderful person who makes me feel special." I was surprised, yes, but not bothered. Mom's business was Mom's business. I didn't want to think about her sex life regardless of the gender of her partner. But Karen had reported that her daughter, Quinn, "who is the same age as Emma and I'm sure they'll be fast friends," took it poorly. There was yelling and screaming and a lot of "how can you do this to me?"

I was a peach by comparison, especially since the only reaction I could manage was, "Her daughter needs to calm down" and "Man, Dad will be pissed." Which she did, and he was, and I predicted all that because I'm smarter than the average bear.

Three months after the big reveal, Mom and I had another sit-down talk because Karen and Quinn were moving in. I hadn't met either of them by that point—Mom had kept her relationship separate so I wouldn't get hit with shrapnel if things went bad. But a romantic week in Aruba and the happy couple determined it was time to take the next big step. I wasn't super excited about living with strangers and I said as much. Mom apologized but it was pretty clear it was going to happen whether or not I liked it. When I told Dad, he offered an open door, but…

I love my dad. It's just that he took the divorce to mean open season on thirty-year-old females. I didn't want to have to deal with seeing him as the Godfather of Skank, nor did I want to be home by myself the rest of the time—he was a pilot and out of town a lot. Stuck between two bad situations, I picked Karen and Quinn.

To this day, I'm not sure that was a smart decision.

The first meeting of the East and West Side lesbian families was "interesting." My mom is short, curvy and olive-skinned thanks to her Sicilian heritage. The hair at her temples is graying, but the rest of it is a beautiful chestnut that hangs to her tailbone. She has round features and her eyes are a pale, pretty brown. She's an art teacher, so she spends a lot of time picking paint and clay out from under her fingernails. Karen is her absolute opposite. Tall, lithe and imposing, she wears suits and carries a briefcase and actually owns more than one pair of high heels. She's a Nordic empress with blond hair, blue eyes and skin so pale she makes paper look tan.

From the moment Karen stepped out of her silver Mercedes with the black leather seats, I was uncomfortable. She was dressed in her version of casual—khakis and a white shirt—but she obviously had money and she comported herself like it. I grew up blue-collar middle class, and seeing her polish made me feel grubby by comparison. I fidgeted as she approached, her capped teeth gleaming in the sun.

"Hi, Emma. I'm Karen. So glad to finally meet you." She flashed a smile before settling into Mom's side. Mom shifted her weight, her cheeks flushed. She was nervous, though I didn't know if that was because I was meeting Karen for the first time or because she was finally meeting Quinn. To Karen's credit, she noticed my mom's discomfort. She grazed her fingers across Mom's biceps. Then she glanced at me to see if the contact freaked me out. I was more impressed that she cared about Mom's welfare than to sweat a display of affection.

"Hey. Hi," I said. "It's… Yeah. Cool."

I sounded like a stammering moron. But what if Karen turned out to be Cruella de Vil? What if she hated me? What if she made my mom unhappier than my dad did after that whole midlife-crisis flight-attendant-humping fiasco?

"Quinn incoming. I'm sure you two will get along," Karen said, motioning at the Mercedes. "She's worried about going to a new high school in the fall."

Karen sounded so very certain, like an Emma-and-Quinn friendship was a preordained thing. I had a momentary flash of hope that Quinn and I could watch *Doctor Who* together or maybe nerd out about CW shows. If she was a reader, I had four bookshelves in my room loaded with comics and trade paperbacks and all The Dark Tower books.

Maybe this won't be so bad, I said to myself. *Maybe it'll be cool.* Then Quinn stepped out of the car. She was perfect. Her strawberry blonde hair hung to her elbows, her skin so flawless it'd make a model weep. I was short, chubby and dark. She was tall, willowy and golden. I wore three-dollar flip-flops. She wore Gucci pumps that cost more than my entire outfit. Her makeup was perfect; my lip balm was a dollar-bin find. I held a book in my hand, she held—

—a purse dog. A Chihuahua, to be exact, that I later found out was named Versace.

She stood there, her mongrel snarling at me like it wanted to eat my face. I hugged my well-loved copy of *Harry Potter and the Prisoner of Azkaban* like it was the last bit of sanity in an insane world. She eyed me, I eyed her and both our faces fell. The universe had conspired to bring high school elite and high school nerd-herd together, and wasn't that hysterical?

"Hi," I said, forcing my lips into something that resembled a smile but probably looked more like I wanted to puke.

"Oh, good. Lesbian is hereditary. Not cool, Mom," Quinn snapped before tromping back to the car, her familiar yapping all the way. She slammed the door and pulled out her phone, her thumbs flying over the screen. She was talking about me already—to people I didn't know. And she thought I was…

"I'm not a lesbian," I said to the Mercedes. I turned around to blink at Karen and Mom. "I'm not a lesbian," I repeated stupidly. It wasn't that I minded the misperception, but I felt a need to clarify for Karen's sake. Or maybe I wanted to say something that wasn't, "Wow, Karen. Your daughter sucks."

Karen groaned and ran a hand down her face, her gaze swinging up to the summer sky. "I am so sorry. She's taking this poorly."

From that point on, so was I.

CHAPTER TWO

KAREN AND QUINN MOVED IN JUST BEFORE MY JUNIOR year started. Quinn sulked, brooded, complained and was an all-around Misery Princess for the first week. Day eight was when my raging hate-on for her was born. She'd started the day with, "Girls are supposed to have two boobs, not one. Get a bra that fits," over breakfast, and that was annoying, but it wasn't a deal breaker. The conversation I overheard with her father later in the day, however, was another story.

My mother had worked hard to make Quinn feel welcome. The month before Quinn and Karen's arrival, Mom painted Quinn's new bedroom Quinn's favorite color, refinished her floor to beautiful hardwood and bought her a new, expensive bedroom set. She'd stocked the house with Quinn's favorite foods, and cleared space for her in the upstairs bathroom. She bought her a desktop computer so Quinn could do her homework with relative ease, and even added Quinn to the car insurance so Quinn could take advantage of her driver's permit.

Mom cared. She showed it by asking Karen every day, multiple times a day, how she could help make Quinn's transition easier. She treated Quinn like a VIP, buying her iced coffees and ice cream sundaes that Quinn would reject on account of calories. Whenever Quinn emerged from her Quinn hole, Mom was at her beck and call.

Through all of it, Quinn remained…*aloof* was probably the nice way of putting it, but she was cold, and sharp, and dismissive. She never showed any signs of appreciation. She took and took and took and offered nothing in return, which was why when I heard her slamming my mother when she was on the phone, I wanted to put her head through the wall.

"I hate it here," she said. "It's awful."

I was passing by her room when she said that, the thin door not enough to keep her voice contained. I paused even though I knew I'd regret it, and she continued. "Emma, Dana's daughter, is boring and fat. This house is ghetto, this town is gross. Dana got her lesbian all over Mom and I want to puke whenever they touch each other. Like, keep your gay to yourself, please."

It was stupid, awful and bigoted. It was also crap; neither of our mothers was demonstrative, probably because they wanted us to be comfortable and their relationship was still new to us. Quinn was making stuff up to her father. I shook my head and rolled my eyes, about to head back to my room, when she said, "I don't even dare wear shorts around here. Dana's constantly checking me out."

Oh, no. Nope, not today, Satan.

"My mother's not a pedo," I snapped, slapping hard on Quinn's closed door. "And she's been nothing but nice to you. If you're going to lie, at least do it where someone can't call you on your crap."

"I gotta go, Dad." Something smacked against the wall and I heard her stomping my way. I stepped back right as she pulled open her door, her eyes narrowed to slits, her hair tied up on top of her head in a sloppy bun. She wore one of those tank tops that showed off a belly button ring and a pair of pink and blue checkered pajama pants.

"Don't listen to my phone conversations!" she screamed in my face, a spray of spittle striking my cheeks.

I winced and wiped my face, my jaw grinding. "The walls are thin. And don't pretend me overhearing you calling my mother a pedophile is somehow worse than you saying it in the first place."

"You're standing outside of my door, you fat bitch. Don't even!" Behind her, Versace snarled like he was Cerberus guarding the gates of Hell. I eyed him, he eyed me back and then he charged. Quinn could have stopped him, easily in fact, but she moved aside to let him come at me, the little turd of a dog darting in to attack. Razor-sharp teeth tore into my skin, Versace's head worrying back and forth when he got a good grip on me. I yelped and punted the little jerk to get him off me.

He hit the wall with a thud and a whine.

Quinn flew out of her room to scoop up her teeth-gnashing baby, checking him for lingering injury. She assessed him for damage, bending all of his limbs to ensure I hadn't snapped them in half like an ogress.

"Oh my God. Stay the hell away from my dog! Ugh, you are such a bitch!" I stared at her in horror, rivulets of blood streaking down my bare foot to stain the rug below. I was so mad I thought I'd rip her hair out, but hearing the kerfuffle, both of our moms crested the stairs to intervene, Karen stepping between us. She herded Quinn back into her bedroom while my mom took me to the bathroom to bandage my foot.

Mom shut the door to tune out the screeching harpy next door.

"Are you okay?" She sat on the edge of the tub, pulling my foot into her lap. It wasn't so awful—a few puncture wounds, a scratch. Thankfully Versace wasn't a German shepherd, though my ankle throbbed something fierce. Chihuahua teeth are no joke.

"Would you be? Her dog bites me and I'm the asshole."

"Language," Mom chastised. Right, language. Because that was the important part. But being snide wasn't going to help my cause, and so I sat on the toilet, looking at the countertop. Quinn had commandeered it from day one, multiple baskets holding her lotions and potions and skin care. There were trays for her makeup, bins for her feminine products and EpiPens, and a cup holding combs and hairbrushes. The upstairs bathroom used to be mine, but her stuff was a flag staked into the ground, claiming that six-by-eleven space for the nation of Quinn.

Can I secede? Please?

Mom dabbed at my cuts with hydrogen peroxide. "She'll calm down. Karen says Quinn's struggled with the separation." Mom glanced up from her doctoring, strain lines framing her eyes and mouth. "I know she's being difficult, but we can give her a chance to settle in before we call it a wash, right?"

"She just told her father on the phone you were checking her out," I said. "I'm not sure she deserves a chance."

That stopped her cold, and she peered up at me from behind her dark brows. Her mouth did a pucker thing, her shoulders tensed and she sighed. "I'll talk to Karen, but the point remains. She's having a hard time. Let's be the bigger people."

Whatever.

"If the dog bites me again I want it gone," I added as an afterthought. "I don't need to be mauled in my own home."

Mom nodded and reached for the Band-Aids. "That's fair. Maybe we'll get him a muzzle."

Can we get one for Quinn, too?

Nah, I'm not that lucky.

The damage went deeper than the bite marks. Quinn was such a problem child, I secretly hoped Mom and Karen would break up. I knew it wouldn't happen—they were far too happy—but my peaceful home was in tatters as a result of their relationship. As a result of *Quinn*. Mom kept assuring me that Quinn was adapting and to be patient, but I knew what evil lurked behind that bedroom door. A bona fide bitch. And bitches kept right on bitching because that was their basic bitch function.

Quinn threw the curveball our first day of school. I went downstairs in my jeans, sweatshirt and wet hair, expecting attitude, but she was smiling at the breakfast table. Rare. And conversational. Rarer. For the briefest moment, I wondered if maybe Mom was right. Maybe Quinn had purged the douche bag demon festering inside. Or maybe her fairy godmother had granted her a modicum of decency sometime during the night.

"You have good hair, Emma. Like, a nice color and it's long. You should wear it down," she said.

I blinked at her over my wobbly pile of scrambled eggs, expecting a second head to sprout from her neck. She smiled. I glanced over at my mother, who was hovering by the sink. Mom and I shared a look. She nodded, encouraging me to say something equally accommodating. It took me a minute to get over my opossum-in-headlights shock, but after a couple of bites I managed, "Thanks. I've been growing it out."

"You can use my flat iron to straighten it before school if you want. Tomorrow or whatever."

"Oh. Cool." I had no idea how to use a flat iron, but I wasn't going to tell her that. I apparently didn't need to, either.

"...I'll show you later. After school."

"Oh. Thanks."

One morning of her being nice didn't assuage the pain of our introductory weeks, but it did shake my resolve to hate her with the fury of a thousand suns. The whole time we waited for the bus, she chattered about how she missed her old friends and how much a new school terrified her. I mustered some sympathy for her that day. Actually, I maintained that sympathy the first week of school because she was nice to me. In turn, I introduced her to everyone I knew because that's what you did when you had the new kid on your hip.

I wasn't so stupid as to think that we were going to be best friends, but she was tolerable enough that I thought *maybe* we could coexist amicably. I was even encouraged when I found out we were going to be in the same art class. Quinn liked photography and I slanted toward sketching and inking, but art was a common interest.

The first day of art class, she took the seat next to me. The way the classroom was set up, there were four double rows of black tables, each one big enough for three workstations. I sat at the end, Quinn took the middle and, right as the bell rang, Nikki Lambert came running into the room, her hair dyed pink and gray and purple, to take the third seat. She wore a black shirt, a short black skirt, black-and-white striped tights and a pair of black combat boots. She was a punk rock chick with runway style, cool in that outcast "too mature for the rest of us" way. She and I weren't super close friends, but we'd hung out a bit during sophomore year and over the summer, and I liked her a lot.

"Hi, I'm new. Quinn Littleton," Quinn said as an opener. "I'm Emma's— My mom's dating Emma's mom, so we're like sisters living in lesbian land."

Nikki dropped a camouflage bag with a red anarchy symbol embroidered on the side onto the table. Her eyebrows lifted as she looked between me and Quinn, a weird smile playing around her mouth. Her lip piercing gleamed silver as she wriggled it around with her tongue.

"I'm Nikki." Nikki waved at me and I noticed that each of her fingernails was painted a different color. I thought it was awesome. So did Quinn. She reached out to take Nikki's hand, pulling it close to admire it.

"The gray is Opi, yeah?"

Nikki peered at her for a long moment, not snatching her hand away but clearly surprised by Quinn's friendliness. So was I. I never would have had the guts to be so outgoing with a stranger.

"Yeah. I think so," Nikki said.

"I love their stuff. I'm such a nail polish whore."

They shared a look that I couldn't quite read. Before anything else could be said, our teacher, Mr. Riddell, walked in. He always looked like he smelled something foul—his brow was knitted with worry lines, his nostrils were pinched, his mouth was flat and wide like a guppy's. Even his smiles looked pained. But the better I got to know him, the more I understood that this wasn't an indicator of bad disposition. Nature had given Mr. Riddell a resting sad face.

"Welcome, everybody," he said. "I'm looking forward to a creative year!"

We didn't do any art that day, just got a tour of the classroom to see where all our supplies were kept. Mr. Riddell talked about his syllabus and asked us what we'd like to focus on for the year. It was the standard first-day stuff. By the time the bell rang, I was eager to get started but that'd have to wait another day. I stooped over to grab my book bag, and when I stood, there was Quinn, a grin on her face.

"Mind if I invite Nikki to lunch?"

"We're having lunch together?" I blinked stupidly.

Quinn smirked. "Yeah. Why wouldn't we?"

I nodded despite the *because you hated me two days ago* rattling around inside my brain. "I don't mind. She's pretty cool."

"Nice. I'll ask."

And I watched as Quinn dazzled her way into Nikki's charms. She made it look so easy, like people were puzzles she had no problem solving. I should have realized then that this was indicative of a lot of experience. I should have realized that only a person who cycled through friends would know how to ingratiate herself so well so quickly.

Live and learn.

Not only did Nikki eat with us that day, she ate with us every day that week. I'd taken up my usual seat between my two best friends at the time, Laney Rosenberg and Tommy Naughters. Quinn sat across from me with Nikki to her side. They kept to themselves, giggling and whispering, so it was no big surprise when Quinn informed me that Nikki would be coming home with us after school that day. I thought it was neat that Quinn had already made a friend. Nikki clearly thought it was neat, too.

I had no idea exactly how *neat* things had gotten.

At the house, the two of them disappeared into Quinn's room. I was disappointed at being relegated to third wheel, but I settled in at the kitchen table and let my mountain of homework keep me busy instead of brooding about being ignored. Every so often a peal of laughter would ripple downstairs, but that stopped fairly quickly. They were so silent, I almost forgot they were there until Karen called at half past four sounding out of breath.

"Hi, Emma. Quinn about?" she asked.

"She's in her room."

"Can you get her for me? I need to ask her a question so I can schedule her allergist appointment."

I mumbled a yes and trod upstairs, wary of a Versace attack as I rapped my knuckles on Quinn's door. She hadn't quite latched it so it swung open with barely any pressure on my part. The Chihuahua immediately started doing his angry Chihuahua thing from his bed in the corner, and I glanced at it, but then Quinn let out a squeal. My eyes flew to her double bed with its white canopy. I blinked. I blinked twice. It took a moment to register what I was seeing, but when I did, I couldn't unsee it.

There was Quinn, naked as the day she was born, with Nikki doing *stuff* to her.

Quinn grabbed a pillow and hugged it to her chest to cover her boobs, Nikki lifted her head in a panic, the dog scrambled to his feet and ran at me like he'd maul me from the knees down. Something clicked on in my brain telling me I should extricate from the situation before a Chihuahua devoured me, so I closed the door, my hand resting on the knob, the flat pane of white wood a blur before my face. All the while, the phone in my grasp called my name over and over again.

Finally, Karen's voice penetrated the *yeah, I totally saw that* stupor, and I lifted the phone to my ear again.

"She's uhh…indisposed," I said.

Lame, yes, but I was pretty sure telling Karen her kid was having sex in the other room would do no one any favors—least of all me. I already wanted to remove my brain from my skull and give it a solid bleaching.

Karen sounded alarmed. "Everything all right? I heard her shout."

"Yeah. She's—" I struggled for the right words as Quinn and Nikki hissed furiously to one another on the other side of the bedroom door "—she's fine. She was getting changed. I surprised her."

"Oh! Yikes. Okay. Right. Well, tell her to call my cell. I have a dinner appointment at five so I won't be available after that, but—thanks, Emma."

"You're welcome," I said. I went back downstairs, my face burning fire. What was I supposed to say to either of them when they emerged? "Sorry I interrupted your sex?" or maybe "Gee, Quinn, maybe being a lesbian is contagious after all?" We'd had peace around the house since school started, but that was probably out the window. Quinn was undoubtedly going to hate me for…

"Hey, Emma?"

Her voice wasn't angry.

My spine stiffened all the same. "Yeah?"

"I'm really sorry ab—you know. That." I glanced up to see her leaning over the railing of the stairs in a T-shirt and pair of shorts. She was flushed, though whether that was embarrassment or sex glow, I didn't know. Nikki appeared behind her, her anarchy bag slung over her shoulder, her colorful hair disheveled. She was red in the face, and she barely looked at me as she darted outside, muttering a goodbye before the door slammed in her wake.

Being caught inside my stepsister embarrassed her. I couldn't say I blamed her for that.

"Crap. I can follow her if you want," I said, feeling guilty Nikki was so weirded out.

"No, it's— I'll call her later. It's cool. But don't say anything to anyone, okay? It's nothing serious. I'm just messing around." Quinn jostled her weight back and forth, her hands fluffing out her hair. "It's not like I'm gay. I was getting off. But you don't want that kind of stuff getting around school."

I nodded dumbly at her, and then kept nodding when she returned to her room. I had no intention of saying anything to anyone, especially not our moms who weren't going to take that last comment all that well. No, I'd keep my mouth shut and hope that it'd all go away.

Except it didn't. It really, really didn't.

Quinn lay low all that night through the next morning. When I came down for breakfast, she was quiet, tossing me a half smile but offering none of the friendly-ish chatter of the last few days. The wait for the bus was silent. Walking into school was silent. It put me on edge, but I tried chalking it up to a bad day or late-breaking awkwardness that I'd seen her being intimate with someone.

No, it wasn't at all a sign that the dark times returneth.

I passed Nikki in the hall once and she met my eyes for a brief second before jerking her gaze away. She scampered into her classroom, head down. And when art class came I sat down at my station beside Quinn only to watch Nikki park herself at another table across the room, as far away from the two of us as possible.

"What's that all about?" I asked under my breath.

"She's mad," Quinn said matter-of-factly.

"Why? What'd you do?"

"Nothing! She's mad I won't be her girlfriend. I'm about the pole, not the hole. Silly dyke."

There were multiple problems with the answer. The first was her tone—it was grade A snark, the likes of which I hadn't seen since before school started. It was enough to put my body into fight-or-flight mode: my palms went clammy, my stomach clenched. I wanted to dive under a rock to get away from such concentrated meanness.

The second was the context. Nikki had definitely not been holding Quinn down. In fact, one of Quinn's legs had been firmly propped on Nikki's shoulder, which was not an indicator that Quinn had been forced into anything. Nikki might have instigated it, but it was hypocritical to call someone a "silly dyke" when you were a willing participant in your very queer sex.

The last problem—and by far the biggest problem—was her volume. I'd whispered my question but Quinn had responded loudly. Loudly enough that everyone looked at her, then over to Nikki, and back again, knowing exactly who Quinn was talking about. The color drained from Nikki's face as she looked at the class, her eyes enormous.

She'd been outed. Publicly. In a conservative high school with a whopping No One out of the closet. Westvale was gossipy, and very, very white, and very, very privileged. The fact that no one had burned rainbow crosses on my front lawn when Karen moved in was nigh miraculous.

"Stop looking at me," Nikki snarled, her hand fisting in the straps of her bag before she ran for the door. She collided with Mr. Riddell as he walked in; he *oomph*ed and called her name, but Nikki kept running, not to be seen again for four days.

CHAPTER THREE

ART CLASS STARTED AS THE SOLE THING QUINN AND I shared in common, but quickly morphed into "the hour I spend with that chick I abhor." Her stock rose after she screwed over Nikki. People were curious about her. A handful of people called her homophobic, yes, but others justified her behavior, saying it was Nikki's fault for hitting on a straight girl in the first place. Far more people applauded Quinn's "bravery" than condemned her insensitivity, which was all sorts of messed up.

I wondered how the perception would have changed if Nikki told everyone the truth. I had no issue with Quinn identifying as straight and screwing a girl—plenty of gay folks had straight sex, and experimentation was a legit thing. But Quinn was cruel when she talked about the gay people in her circle. Even if she hadn't been getting her hump on with Nikki, look at her mother, at *our* mothers, and how she'd accused my mother of inappropriate staring. How could she be so horrible?

I stewed about it for days. The conclusions I reached weren't heartening. Even if Nikki set the record straight, Quinn couldn't lose. Most of the guys in my school would have been more interested in the fap material than the injustice of what Quinn did to Nikki. Quinn would go from being the hot, interesting new girl to the walking boner fodder of Westvale.

The only thing I could do was extend an olive branch to Nikki. Her first day back after her hiatus, I found her at lunch. I was so nervous, I got slimy-sweaty and worried about pit stains. A few deep breaths, a few prayers to my benevolent, godly maker, and I approached her table, my lunch tray clasped tight between my hands. She stopped eating her pudding midspoonful. Her expression was empty, like this was a stranger wearing a Nikki mask and not the girl herself.

"What Quinn did was wrong and I'm sorry." I couldn't look her in the eye so I concentrated on the rhinestone barrettes in her hair instead. "If you want to tell people that she's a liar, I'll back you up. That wasn't cool."

I expected her to tell me to screw off, but after a long pause, she kicked out the empty chair across from her in invitation.

"Not worth it," she said, returning her attention to her pudding.

I ate with Nikki every day after that, Tommy and Laney joining us to round out our quartet. It marked the last day of the Quinn/Emma alliance. Quinn didn't need me anymore. Derek Powers, our star baseball player, asked her out after Nikki's shamefest and that was it—Quinn had her "in" with the popular kids. She was free to blossom from a petulant, pain-in-the-butt bud to a full-blown terror flower.

My home life deteriorated to its previous misery while school was "pretend the other one is dead" time. The hostility made art class a chore. Quinn would walk in, see where Nikki sat, and purposefully take the workbench farthest away. I stuck with Nikki so that put me and Quinn on opposite ends of the classroom. One day, while I was sketching, I told Nikki that it was an apt metaphor for my and Quinn's relationship as a whole—a nation divided, ne'er the twain shall meet.

"Cool," Nikki said. "Glad I'm on the non–douche bag side of the Mason-Dixon."

So was I.

A week later, Quinn's trouble with Mr. Riddell started. Once Quinn got popular, she got social. Really social. Our school had a policy that cell phones had to be put away at all times or they would be confiscated. Either Quinn thought she could charm her way out of punishment or didn't think the rules applied to her in the first place.

That was a mistake.

It was a Tuesday, and we were working with watercolors. The exercise was to blend the paints as seamlessly as possible. It wasn't difficult, but apparently it wasn't interesting enough for Quinn. I could see her in the front row. She alternated between twisting the paintbrush between her fingers and reaching into her bag to pull out her phone. Every time Mr. Riddell patrolled to look at work, she'd thrust her hands under the table or put the phone away, but Mr. Riddell wasn't an idiot.

"Focus on the work, Miss Littleton. Not whatever it is you're doing over there."

"Uh-huh." She flashed him an oopsie smile, probably hoping her revolting cuteness would sway him, before picking up the paintbrush and doing three swirls across her paper. The moment he walked out of her row, she was back at the phone, her head pointed down, her shoulders hunched so she could hide when Riddell patrolled near. To use my dad's saying, it was as subtle as a fart in church.

"Dumbass," Nikki muttered to me under her breath.

"Yep."

Three more circuits through the room, two more warnings from the teacher before Mr. Riddell got tired of Quinn's crap. He didn't come at her from the front row, but from the row behind. Quinn had her head down, her thumbs flying when he reached over her shoulder to pluck the phone from her grasp. She yelped and whirled around, trying to snatch it from his ham fist, but Riddell shook his head and headed toward his desk, depositing the phone in his top drawer.

"You may retrieve it at the end of the school day," he said.

Quinn's ears went pink. It wasn't shame—she wasn't really capable of shame—so much as annoyed exasperation. "What if there's an emergency? Like, a school shooter. There's a billion trench coat kids here. Tommy Nutters has crazy eyes. Hello?"

Tommy Naughters may have been my ex-boyfriend, but he was still my friend. I glowered at the back of her head, wishing I had heat-ray vision. Sadly, my lack of superpowers meant her strawberry blondeness didn't erupt into flames.

Mr. Riddell grimaced. "Back to work, Quinn."

"But…"

"Multiple warnings to put it away means no buts. You may collect the phone at the end of the day. If that doesn't suit you, I can give it to the principal's office and they can call your mother to collect it for you."

Quinn's pink face went red. This was a telltale precursor of Quinn having a fit, which at home resulted in headaches and new designer purses from Karen. I almost hoped she'd lose it in class so I could snicker about her rotting in detention for the rest of her natural life, but a pat on the shoulder from Drone A on her left calmed her enough that she kept her trap shut.

"Whatever," she snapped, slamming her paintbrush down on her worktable.

Okay, *mostly* kept her mouth shut.

Class was unremarkable after that. Quinn was sullen. The watercolors were watercolors and did what watercolors do, which wasn't much. By the time the bell rang, Quinn had worked herself into a snit. She grabbed her books and stormed toward Mr. Riddell's desk, one hand perched on her hip, her shoe tapping against the tile floor.

"Can I have it now? My last class is across the building and I have plans after school."

Mr. Riddell made a show of stacking his papers in a neat pile. "This will be the third time you've pushed me, so no, you may not. And now your choice is to pick it up tomorrow after school or I'll call your mother to pick it up today."

"Come *on*! I'm expecting a call from my dad later. Please?"

I'd been easing my way toward the door when Quinn's wail stopped me short. Nikki was at my elbow, and she leaned back so she had a clear view of Riddell's desk. He didn't seem all that concerned with Quinn's plea or the multiple eyes watching the unfurling drama.

"No. Tomorrow or your mother. Which is it?"

"This is so stupid." Quinn marched for the door, grumbling under her breath the entire time. She was about out of the classroom when Mr. Riddell called her name. She turned, eyes bulging with barely suppressed rage. I sensed the imminent threat of combustion. The art room easels would be strewed with glittery entrails, lacy underwear and Midol.

"Which is it, Quinn? That wasn't rhetorical." At Quinn's blank stare because rhetorical had too many syllables, Mr. Riddell sank into his computer seat, his hand drumming on the desktop. "Tomorrow, or should I call your mother today?"

"Tomorrow," she spat, her temper barely in check as she stomped her way into the hall. Nikki and I shared a look and headed out, both of us thinking Quinn would get her phone back tomorrow and that'd be it.

Noooooope.

Quinn avoided Mr. Riddell calling home so she could deliver her own slant to her mother after school. She made it sound like Mr. Riddell had screamed at her mercilessly before amputating the arm attached to the phone. The complaining went on for hours, Quinn saying what a jerk Mr. Riddell was and how boring class had been so, really, it was his fault that she'd been texting in the first place. She actually screeched in rage because she had to use something as archaic as the house phone. It couldn't even look at the internet, she reminded us, and she had to go all the way upstairs to check her Instagram on her computer! And *how stupid was that? OH MY GOD!*

How we survived her hissy fit is a wonder. It probably had something to do with Karen getting Quinn out of the house at dinnertime so no one accidentally impaled her in the forehead with a butter knife. And by "accidentally," I mean totally on purpose because the whining made me crazy.

"She's going to buy her off, you realize," I said to my mother after they left. Mom gave me a look for stating the obvious, but sure enough, two hours later Quinn walked in with a dress bag in one hand and an ice cream sundae in the other. My mom gave Karen the hairy eyeball for it, but there were certain battles she wouldn't pick. Karen's lackluster conflict-management skills was one of them.

Quinn got her phone back the next day and was, by all appearances, properly chastened. If she was a sane person, that would have been the end of it, but no. A week after the confiscation, Mr. Riddell made the tragic mistake of coming to school sick. He was pink and sweaty and clearly uncomfortable. I was guessing he was feverish because he took off his vest, his tie and divested himself of the stuff in his pockets, like the extra weight made him hotter. Halfway through class, while we painted watercolor animals, he excused himself and rushed out the door for the bathroom. This wasn't noteworthy until Quinn noticed Mr. Riddell's phone on the corner of his desk.

"Oh. Oh, ho," Quinn said, standing. She whispered to the girl next to her, Melody Cohler, who was in the larval stages of BFFness. Melody's scandalized giggles spurred Quinn onward. Quinn sauntered over to the phone, and by the utter joy spreading across her face, I could tell Mr. Riddell hadn't password protected it. Her thumbs flew over the keypad before she paused and eyed the door, her smile turning feline.

I glanced at Nikki. She scowled at Quinn's back. And then she was sitting up straighter in her chair, her mouth falling open. I followed her gaze and then *my* mouth fell open. Quinn was in the corner lifting her shirt, snapping off selfies of her boobs with Mr. Riddell's phone.

"What the crap are you doing?" I asked because no one else in the class could articulate. They were all too stunned to speak.

"Stay out of it, Emma," she replied as she took more pictures from the side view. My classmates started snickering, and one of the guys in the back made whooping noises, but Quinn spun around to stab a talon in his direction. "Shut up, Aidan. Everyone shut up or I swear I will kick your asses. This is between me and Riddell."

Quinn took some less risqué pictures. There was a picture of a vase and some art on the walls, a few shots of the paintbrushes drying on the window ledge. I didn't understand why until Nikki snorted, looking down at her half-finished painting of a goat. Other people painted pandas or parrots or ponies, but my new best friend picked a goat. Because she was weird.

"She's burying the pictures. This can't go well for him," she said.

The ramifications didn't occur to me when Quinn returned the phone to the desk. Nor did they occur to me when I went home from school. No, I didn't quite *get it* until the next Monday when I walked into art class. Standing at the front of the room was a woman who couldn't have been more than twenty-six or twenty-seven with Principal Ahadi at her side.

"Everyone, this is Miss Glass. She'll be taking over for Mr. Riddell for the foreseeable future. I assure you, you're in great hands. Any questions, you know where to find me."

My stomach dropped to the floor.

She ratted him out. Those pictures got out, or she told someone about them or forwarded them and now he's gone.

I didn't want to believe that Quinn could be so catty as to compromise a guy's job for scolding her, but when I saw her sit back in her seat in the front row, her arms folding over her chest, her smugness a living, breathing thing threatening to gobble all the space in the classroom, I knew she was responsible.

"Oh. Oh, wow," I whispered, sinking into my seat, my face flushing hot. "I cannot believe she did that."

Nikki shook her head so hard her silver cross earrings smacked against her cheeks. "I can. That girl makes Hannibal Lecter look like a saint."

CHAPTER FOUR

"IF YOU TELL THE SCHOOL ABOUT THE RIDDELL THING, I'll end you."

One minute I was shoving a bologna sandwich in my face at the kitchen table, a book open before me, the next Quinn loomed over me in her workout pants and tank top like a perfumed vulture.

"That's nice. You're in my light. Move?"

She batted my book away. The pages rustled and settled somewhere in the middle that was distinctly not my place. It irritated me. I was at a really good spot, when Katniss... It's not important. You don't mess with my *The Hunger Games* and she messed with my *The Hunger Games* and for that I wanted to snap her like a twig.

"You don't have to be a dong about it." I snatched the book and tucked it beneath the table where her grimy tentacles couldn't touch it.

"You're not listening to me, Emilia."

This was a new thing, the Emilia bit. I have no idea where she got it from, but it was stupid.

"I am listening. Don't tell anyone about the Riddell thing. Now can I go back to reading?"

"No, see. You don't get me." She leaned down, until her lips were an inch away from my ear, her breath lashing at my skin. I could feel her body heat against my back. "If you tell anyone, I will make you so miserable at school, you'll wish you were dead."

She was threatening me.

Awesome.

Faaaaantastic.

I rubbed the back of my neck, unwilling to admit aloud that her unleashing her winged monkeys scared me to death, but that was the truth of it. I liked my low profile. I liked hanging out with Nikki and Laney and Tommy, and being ignored by my classmates. It was safe. Being Quinn's target dummy outside of the house as well as in? Was the anti-safe. "Whatever, okay? I'll leave it alone."

Satisfied with my cowardice, she wandered off to the bathroom. I heard the radio blare followed by the rush of water. I tossed the book onto the counter and headed out the door, my hand plunging into my jeans pocket in search of my cell phone. Fifteen minutes later, I arrived at the Bouncing Bear Coffee Shop on the corner and Tommy Naughters was pulling into the parking lot in a Jeep Cherokee so old it looked like it was held together with duct tape.

Tommy was an old friend, like since-grade-school old friend. Tall and knobby at the joints, he had dark brown hair and hazel eyes and an Adam's apple that bulged from his neck like he'd swallowed a baseball. He was nerdy like me with his video game T-shirts and black trench coat. We'd dated awhile but it hadn't gone anywhere. Part of that was his propensity for writing emo poetry. I liked him too much to laugh in his face at what was supposed to be a romantic gesture. But know this: I stilled his soul, granting him the respite given only to those in the tomb.

I still giggle thinking about it because I'm a jerk.

The other part was my mad crush on Shawn Willis, a guy so out of my league it wasn't even funny. Every time Shawn walked into a room at school, my mouth went dry and I lost my train of thought. Like, midsentence I'd go silent. Tommy noticed The Shawn Effect. He didn't appreciate it, and our gropey fumblings and makeouts weren't so good he couldn't walk away from them.

We stayed friends despite the split, and things were better than ever with him dating my other friend, Laney. She worked at that particular Bouncing Bear, though Tommy said she had the day off and wouldn't be joining us on account of a family thing. Laney adored Tommy, emo poetry and all, because dead roses were more a goth chick's scene and Laney was all about her pleather and fishnets.

Tommy clambered from the Jeep in his usual coat, jeans and combat boots, a *Dungeons & Dragons* book tucked beneath his arm. Seeing me waiting inside at the corner booth, he waved.

"I got a new adventure for us next week," he said.

"Cool. I'm digging the cleric. Hopefully I won't blow this one up."

One of the common threads of our friendship was a mutual appreciation for tabletop role-playing games. This fact had never and would never make it to Quinn, who would have laughed herself to tears that I was one of *those* kids. My diatribe on how storytelling was an ancient art form celebrated in hundreds of cultures and *Dungeons & Dragons* was simply a modern extension of a time-honored tradition would be wasted on her.

"What happened with the Evil One now?" Tommy sat across from me. I slid him an iced coffee I'd ordered from the woman behind the counter. Tommy would pollute his with a mountain of sugar, but I liked mine black.

As black as my twisted soul, my sweet Ophelia.

Poor Tommy.

"She's threatening me about what happened in art class," I said. "That thing with Riddell I told you about? She says she'll ruin me. I don't know what that means, but I'm guessing she'll tell people stuff about me. Or, well, make stuff up. I'm pretty boring."

Tommy tossed a straw my way, his fingers tracing over the cover of his book. "Were you planning to tell anyone about what happened? Was that even a thing?"

I wasn't sure how to answer that. Had I considered it? Yes. Planned? No, not really. After Quinn screwed over Nikki, I'd rushed to make nice with the girl who would become my best friend. Once again I felt compelled to repair Quinn's damage, but I didn't want it to become a habit. Quinn was Quinn. She owned her asshattery. I could apologize or tattle, but didn't that set a problematic precedent?

And in this case, it would be at the expense of my own neck.

"I dunno, should I?" I swirled my drink around inside the plastic cup. The ice clicked and whooshed against the sides. "I feel like maybe I should because he's not a bad guy, but there were thirty other kids there, too. They could say something and take less of a hit from the inevitable Quinn bomb. She's two doors down from me, you know?"

Tommy nudged my foot with his own.

"There you go. It's not on you to fix her shit. You worry about you. She worries about her. I'm sure it'll work out for Riddell."

"Yeah," I said, nodding my head.

In retrospect, this was not the best advice in the world, but hindsight is always twenty-twenty.

The cosmos decided I was a huge toolbag for keeping my mouth shut because at the mall with Nikki the next week, who did we stumble across but the former art teacher himself. I didn't see him coming, but Nikki did. She and I had just walked out of the shoe store, Nikki the proud new shoe mommy to a pair of knee-high black boots with spiky heels, when she took off down the hall like a bullet. I turned in time to see her approach Mr. Riddell, who was two stores up, his eyes huge behind his glasses.

"Mr. Riddell! How are you?" Nikki asked. I trotted after her, my shopping bag whacking my calf.

Mr. Riddell glanced at me nervously, like I carried Quinn cooties with me that could ruin his life for a second time. He sucked in a breath, his meaty cheeks billowing. "Hello. Yes. I'm sorry to… How are you both doing? I enjoyed having you in my class."

Nikki actually swooped in to hug him. He looked shocked, but then awkwardly patted her shoulder as she pulled away, his tight smile making him look like he had gas.

"I'm good, thanks. We miss you, Mr. Riddell. The new

chick's okay but she brought us back to basics. Like 101 techniques in a 201, you know? It's dumb," Nikki said.

He frowned and adjusted his glasses, the crinkles between his brows looking like a chicken's foot. "I am sorry to hear that. Are you still taking lessons at the museum?"

Nikki nodded. "On weekends. We're working with pastels."

"Excellent. And how are you, Emma?" His head swiveled my way.

Why'd he have to look at me?

"I'm good," I managed over the frog in my throat.

Don't be nice. I don't deserve it. Quinn doesn't deserve it.

He nodded, smiling, as a middle-aged woman called his name from across the concourse. "That's my wife. I should go."

Seeing that woman holding her purse, waiting for her husband, compounded my guilt. *Hard.* Mr. Riddell had lost a job he'd had for years. He was married and probably had a mortgage. And bills. And a lifestyle. All of those things may have been compromised because Quinn Littleton couldn't handle a single day without her stupid goddamned cell phone.

"I'm sorry you had to leave." It escaped before I could think better of it. Nikki winced, but I'd opened that door and I'd reap the consequences for it. Red-faced, I peered at him, my fingers clasped together over my stomach.

"I'm sorry?" he asked.

"For Quinn." I couldn't bring myself to say anything else, but I didn't need to, either. Mr. Riddell's face flushed, his concentration no longer focused on my face but on my shoes.

"I wasn't fired, if that's what you're… There was an investigation after an anonymous tip about improper… I was exonerated." He sucked in a shaky breath. "I chose to step down. I couldn't believe a student would be so hateful." If I thought him looking down was uncomfortable, it was doubly so when he lifted his chin. The bevy of lines on his face made him look ancient, like he had tree bark instead of skin. "I suspected it was her. Did she tell you?"

"No. The class saw her do it."

Mr. Riddell's eyes narrowed. For a horrible moment, I thought he'd shout, but then he did something far worse. He asked me *that* question. You know, the one that makes your guts rot out.

"No one spoke on my behalf?"

"*We wanted to,*" I almost said. "*We liked you way more than Quinn.*" But the words became gobbledygook inside my mouth. The shame was so thick, it was like trying to talk through cotton balls. No, no one said anything because Quinn scared everyone. We were held hostage by a skinny blonde leviathan with a mean streak.

Our silence was damning. Mr. Riddell cleaned his glasses on the bottom hem of his shirt like that was infinitely more important than the two girls standing before him. I caught a momentary flash of white, furry belly before the glasses were replaced. "Well, what's done is done. I'm fine, my reputation is intact. Perhaps next time you'll do differently. Good to see you girls. Goodbye, now."

Before Nikki or I could eke out proper apologies, he crossed the walkway to join his wife, the mall crowd closing in behind him.

I gaped at the spot he'd just occupied. "We let a good man burn," I managed.

A drizzle of eyeliner-stained tears streaked down Nikki's cheeks. She dashed them away like she could rid herself of the evidence. "Yeah. We did. Riddell was a good dude. He got me into that art program. God, I hate Quinn."

CHAPTER FIVE

THINGS SETTLED INTO A ROUTINE OF TERRIBLE AFTER the Riddell incident. Quinn did Quinn, no one took her to task because she terrified them. It got twice as bad after she joined the cheerleading squad; she had a small army of popular girls to back her. Add to that her unmatched capacity to wheedle, bully and charm her way through any situation and you had a disaster in Malone Souliers.

She was the Wicked Witch of Westvale.

I was the lucky girl who got to live with her and her little dog, too.

At least Karen didn't suck. She respected my dedication to my grades, complimenting me with, "You have your head on straight—you're going places in life." She talked to me about college, offering to poke her alma mater after I sent out my applications. Not once did she say that stuff to her own daughter. Quinn's concentration had always been the social spheres of school, not academic achievement, so

Karen praised me, all the while nagging Quinn about her floundering grades.

It was a sore spot begging to become an open wound. Sure enough, at the end of first term, things imploded. I'd made Dean's List with straight A's. Quinn barely passed anything because homework was just not something she was interested in doing. Karen regarded her daughter's report card in much the same way Superman would regard a lump of kryptonite in his Christmas stocking.

"This isn't going to work, Quinn. You want to cheer in college but with these grades, you won't *get into* college. You're going to have to do more. Up the grades, show involvement beyond cheerleading. Prove that you're well-rounded. And don't try to sell me on cheerleading scholarships. Cheerleading doesn't have the sway of football or baseball. If you want college, you're going to have to work for it. I can't do this for you."

Quinn bellowed a whole bunch and stomped off to her room, but the idea of colleges turning her away must have bothered her, because she flounced into my room less than an hour later.

"Does your goth friend still work at Bouncing Bear?"

I offered my best deadly librarian stare over the rims of my glasses.

"Her name is Laney, and yes. Why?"

"I need a job."

I actually laughed. Like, in her face. She looked taken aback, and then she looked pissed. "Stop being a douche. I need a job. You heard my mother. I've got to be well-rounded."

I dropped my chin into my palm so I could maintain uncomfortable eye contact. "The last time Laney came over, you told her it's lucky she found the one necrophiliac in Westvale because no one else would screw a corpse. Why would she get you a job *anywhere*?"

Quinn rolled her eyes, but she must have agreed Laney wasn't a good in because I heard her mutter "Josh" before returning to the foul cocoon from whence she came.

I snorted. If she was going the Josh route, things had taken a dire turn.

Josh Winters was one of those kids who was popular in spite of himself. He was okay-ish looking, was smart-ish, played sports moderately well-ish, and had a good-ish sense of humor. Except he didn't act like he was only *ish* because my classmates pandered to him. Josh had money. Lots of money. His parents owned Bouncing Bear, which started as one shop but had spread like a caffeinated plague. You couldn't walk twelve feet down the street without stumbling upon a Bouncing Bear Coffee Shop with its googly-eyed mascot holding a hot cup of deliciousness.

Josh drove a nice car. He wore the best clothes. He had the biggest house in his neighborhood and was generous with the girls who were kind enough to put out for him. He tended to cycle through the ladies and, at one point, Nikki told me he had so many notches on his belt, his pants were about to fall down. Plenty of girls were more than willing to hop on his junk for a pretty bauble or two.

Quinn eluded his grasp. She'd toy with him and then back out, always blaming her *boyfriend du week* or some other totally avoidable whatever for keeping them apart. The reality was she preferred the pretty boys, but she wasn't so dumb as to permanently burn that bridge. Josh smartened up after a while and went after easier fare, but he maintained an eye on Quinn's pert butt, hoping it'd sashay his way.

If she wanted him to help her get the job, she might have to pay for the favor. The question was with what.

Answer: nothing.

Josh, still vying to insert himself into Quinn's orifices, nudged his father about getting Quinn hired. He would later regret this maneuver, as so many of us regret interactions with Quinn, but at the time he probably figured the hot chick would owe him one so why not.

I could have told him the why-nots at length, but he wouldn't have listened. There were some downfalls to being invisible.

Quinn surprised the family on a Saturday morning wearing a logoed pink polo shirt, a purple visor and tan shorts cut so short, I was pretty sure anyone walking behind her would mistake them for panties. It was ridiculous, especially considering we were due for the first snowfall of the season and she'd freeze to death.

"This uniform is so ugly," she whined, tucking the shirt into her sort-of-shorts. "This pink washes me out."

"I think your ass hanging out is the bigger problem," I said, loud enough for my mother to hear. Mom biffed me on the back of the head, almost causing me to choke on my Cheerios.

"That's God getting back at you." Quinn grabbed her pocketbook. "I'm off. Wish me luck!"

Karen smiled after her. It was rare for Quinn to actually listen to anything her mother said, so it probably felt like a huge victory that this one time, Quinn had taken her advice. Once I stopped hacking on cereal, Mom and I eyed one another warily. And then Mom tittered. It was quiet, but it was enough to get me going, too. The next thing you knew, we were both giggling like idiots. Karen looked confused, but neither one of us wanted to rain on her parade so we kept further commentary to ourselves. Though Mom did whisper to me, "It's good she's not a boy or they'd be able to tell if she's circumcised."

We howled.

I expected Quinn's Bouncing Bear stint not to last, but she stuck with it. For that matter, she practically glowed whenever she came home. She wouldn't lift a finger to help around the house, touch her homework, or do anything that required actual effort beyond cheerleading and doing her nails, but for the first month of her employment, Quinn traipsed off to work with nary a complaint, taking early shifts on Saturdays and Sundays and coming home late—sometimes after dark. It didn't cross me as weird until she missed a cheerleading practice. Melody called the house looking for her, saying that Quinn's phone was turned off, and had we seen her today? The squad needed her.

I was watching a movie with Nikki at the time so I blew Melody off with a quick, "Nope, I'll have her call you," and hung up.

Nikki eyeballed me from behind her copy of *Rolling Stone*.

"Quinn missing a practice is like the Pope missing Sunday Mass, you realize. That chick is all about her spread eagles. I actually mean the sport ones this time."

I cocked my head to the side, thoughtful. Quinn's disposition *was* less hell beast than usual, and lately she was even wearing long pants to work in lieu of short shorts because "someone asked her to." Most days, she'd tell that someone to crap in their hat.

"Something's up," I announced. "Her cell is never off."

Nikki ducked behind her magazine. "Ayep. If she missed cheerleading practice, it's a doozy."

I didn't relish the notion of involving myself in Quinn's screwed-up life, but it was too strange to ignore. On the off chance she was on her way to becoming the next Walter White, I felt compelled to ask. Quinn was a creature of annoying habits. This habit was off the charts.

Nikki took off early that night on account of a date, so I was home alone by the time Quinn rambled in from work. I sat on the couch with a book in one hand and a can of soda in the other. She immediately pulled some of her hair from over her shoulder around front, patting it into place until it covered her neck.

"Hickey, huh?" I asked.

She tsked. "None of your business, *Emilia*."

"Not my business, but if I noticed, your mother will." I put down the book and leaned over the couch arm, sweeping the bangs from my eyes when they fell in front of my glasses. "Okay, so either you're working twelve-hour shifts or you're seeing someone. What's up?"

Quinn rarely engaged in deep thought, so when her face scrunched up and her head tilted to the side, I wasn't sure what I was seeing. Constipation, maybe. Or the beginnings of a stroke. But then she flopped onto the chair beside me, moving in so close I couldn't miss her Eau du Donut: a combination of grease, sugar and hazelnut.

"I'm seeing an older man. Like, way older," she said.

That she had a boyfriend didn't surprise me. That she was seeing an "older man" did but only because she was so very particular with her arm candy. She was also particular about how she presented herself when she went out with people—she always looked great, smelled great. Right then, she had jelly on her shoulder and coffee stains on her pants. Her Romeo must have really liked donuts.

Maybe Quinn was doing Homer Simpson.

"How much older?"

"His forties. He says he loves me. Like, I think I might love him. He makes me feel so… Look what he bought me." She reached into her pocket and produced gold hoop earrings with leafy charms dangling from the bottoms. Emeralds, maybe. Or peridots.

"Are those real?" I admired the pretty before my brain kicked in and told me *this is really wrong.* "Wait. It doesn't matter if they're real. Holy crap. You're seventeen! He's forty-something? That's statutory in this state. Like, he could go to jail."

"That's why you can't say anything. I'm trusting you with this. Don't screw me over. Please. I'm happy and I don't want to ruin it."

My tongue twisted. This guy was as old as her dad, which maybe was the point. Was this some Electra complex manifesting? A result of neglect? Her dad rarely called, and when he did, it was for five or ten minutes before he was making his excuses. Heck, my dad flew planes back and forth to Dubai for rich businessmen but I still heard from him once a week.

I rubbed the heel of my palm against my temple. It was a

lot to take in, and nothing I could say would make any of it better. Quinn did the strangest thing then—she reached for me, her pointy fingernails digging into the back of my hand.

"Promise me," she demanded. "Please? I love him."

It was the *please* that got me. For all Quinn's faults, she rarely asked me for anything. True, that was because she either didn't like to acknowledge I was alive or was too busy torturing me to want or need stuff, but she hadn't come to me so much as I'd gone to her. I'd inserted myself and it'd be a bad showing to screw her over with it.

She gave my hand another squeeze.

I groaned in defeat.

"Fine. I promise I won't say anything. But I'm going on the record here. It's creepy and you should be careful."

"I will," she promised. And for the first and last time in my life, Quinn pulled me into a hug. Despite all expectations otherwise, lightning did not strike me dead.

Quinn's spring/winter romance continued for another three weeks. She didn't miss any more practices, but she did spend her weekend days exchanging bodily fluids with her mysterious dude and, in turn, collecting valuable prizes. A necklace. New lingerie. An iPad. She tried to give me the sordid details once, showing me the rug burn she got from Old Boyfriend's car upholstery, but I declined story time, telling her there weren't enough therapists to fix my tender brain meats if she continued talking.

She laughed and called me childish. I was okay with that.

Sadly for Quinn, the Bella and Edward of donuts were

not to be. Quinn came home on a Thursday night slinging curses that would have made a sailor blush. I was playing video games at the time with my noise-canceling headphones on, but somehow, Quinn's banshee wails trumped soundproofing technology.

I went downstairs to check on her only to see her chuck the Bouncing Bear hat across the kitchen.

"I hate him! I hate him! I am… I hate him so much!"

"Are you okay?"

"Leave me alone!"

"Good talk! Leaving you alone." I returned to my virtual playground where, unlike my kitchen, demolitions were an acceptable form of problem solving. Ten minutes later, a wet, bathrobe-clad Quinn haunted my threshold.

"I hate him so much." She threw herself at my bed, muffling her shriek of rage in my Domo-kun pillow. I paused the game and waited. She'd stop leaking her psycho all over my stuff eventually, and I was guessing she'd want to talk at that point.

It took her a few minutes to collect herself. She lifted her head, looked at the fuzzy brown monster with fangs who'd been her tissue, and flung it across the room. Poor Domo-kun. Reduced to a snot rag and discarded.

"S-so he says he can't leave his wife. That they've been together too long. I thought he loved me," she warbled. It was clear by the jut of her chin she was on the verge of sobbing.

Raw emotion from a goodness vacuum such as Quinn Littleton was not an eventuality I was prepared for.

"Aren't you going to say something?" she demanded.

"I… Yeah. I'm sorry you're hurt." I didn't know how to

navigate these waters. I could handle Quinn when she was in typical mean girl mode because that's what I knew. That was her modus operandi. This vulnerable, softer-side-of-Sears Quinn threw me off guard. She looked so fragile and human.

I sucked in a breath. "He didn't deserve you. Plus, when he's sixty you'll be thirty. There's not enough Viagra in the world to cover that."

I didn't expect her to appreciate what I'd said, but she smiled, rolling onto her back to look at my ceiling. "He said he loved me."

"Of course he did. He wanted to do you. It's the oldest cliché in the book." Her expression turned far less friendly. I hadn't meant to criticize her, only I guess I had by suggesting she'd let herself be taken advantage of. I winced. "You know what else is an old cliché? A woman scorned. You'll do better now. Better than him."

"A woman scorned," she repeated.

She lifted her butt off my bed to pull her phone from the pocket of her robe. Her thumbs flew. I glanced over to her screen only to see a picture of Quinn with a silver-tipped head jammed between her ample boobies while she grinned at the camera. Then there was another picture that…okay, that was a nipple. I didn't need to see that, so I looked away. I hadn't signed on for sisterly areolas.

Quinn kept typing.

"He wants to dump me? Whatever. You're right. I will do better. But while I'm doing better, I'm going to make sure he has the worst day of his life."

"What are you doing?" I asked.

Quinn paused to smirk at me, one brow lifted, her eyes

full of flint. "Texting his wife. She really ought to know what he's doing behind her back. A woman scorned, right?"

"Oh," I said. Because what else could I say? I'd fed fire to the fire god. The inferno was a foregone conclusion.

CHAPTER SIX

IT NEVER OCCURRED TO ME THAT QUINN SHOULDN'T have the cell number of her ex-dude's wife. The house phone would have made sense, but she said she was texting Mrs. Cheated On. Unless the married couple shared a cell…

Naaaaah. It was much more convoluted than that.

I went over Nikki's house to hang out with her, Laney and Tommy for Shitty Movie Night. It was a thing we did the first Friday of every month wherein we found the dumbest movie on Netflix, ordered pizza, drank gallons of soda and mercilessly mocked the film. We were buzzards on a fresh corpse. It was great.

It *is* great. We still do it.

We were at the "waiting for the pizza guy to show up" portion of the night, laying siege to Nikki's downstairs family room with the surround sound, big-screen TV and comfortable leather theater seating, when Quinn came up in conversation, albeit in a roundabout way.

"Big goings-on at the Bear," Laney said, sprawled across

Tommy's lap, her heels perched on the armrest of the couch. Her black lips, pale powdered skin and straight black hair made her look especially Morticia, which was a compliment by Laney's standards.

"What's up?" Nikki was painting her toenails rainbow colors, a weird pink foamy thing separating her toes so she didn't smudge. Her glittery lacquer matched her neon skull leggings. Looking between her and Laney, I felt like the only girl present who couldn't be in a rock band. I was relegated to nerdy groupie or maybe, if I was lucky, band manager.

I was still doing better than Tommy, though. He'd be the sound guy.

"The big boss got caught dipping into the employee tip jar if you know what I mean. That's six people now, I think? Mrs. Winters is still around the shop, crabbier than usual, but Mr. Winters is nowhere to be found. I think she's going to take him up the river."

I said nothing because *why didn't that occur to me before? Josh's dad, Quinn? Holy crap!*

"He messed around with Theresa what's-her-name." Nikki capped off her polish, fanning her toes with the menu from the pizza place. "How do you think she got that car? She told her parents she won it in a contest from the chain. Mr. Winters is as nasty as Josh."

"I can't even," I managed. "Gross. So, so, so gross."

Tommy connected the dots first, and his expression—lip curled up on one side in horror, nose crinkled—mirrored my own.

"Oh, crap. Quinn?"

I nodded. "Yeah. She said she loved him. I… Man. I didn't even think about it at the time."

I felt sick. I didn't exactly like Quinn, but for her to fall prey to a serial teen-banger was bad business. She'd told his wife, but it should have gone way beyond that, especially considering Mr. Winters was indiscreet enough in his doings that everyone knew about them.

Well, except for Mrs. Winters.

Until recently.

"Maybe I can convince her to press charges. It *is* statutory," I said.

"She should. Damn. Poor Josh." Tommy flinched. "Poor girls for being used, but that sucks for him, too."

"Especially since he got Quinn the job," Laney added. "Can you imagine if he finds out who outed his father?"

I could, despite not wanting to.

The room grew silent. No one was supposed to ever feel sorry for Quinn Littleton and yet none of us could help it. If she'd known, she would have lost her mind; pity wasn't Quinn's thing. Owning every situation, pretending she was always in charge—that was her deal. Which meant no matter what I said to her about how wrong Mr. Winters had been, she wouldn't press charges. She'd have to tell strangers intimate things that would make her look like she'd been taken advantage of by an older man.

It'd never happen.

Tommy rubbed the back of his neck. Nikki eyeballed her drying toenails. Laney focused on the blank TV screen. The discussion had been a joy vacuum. Fortunately, the doorbell rang with its promise of pizza.

"I've got it," I said, desperate to think about anything that wasn't Quinn. I trotted downstairs, opened the door and then stared. Like a creeper. Because the most beautiful boy in the world stood on the doorstep holding delicious food and Pepsi.

I'd loved Shawn Willis for years. Or, well, not loved, but crushed on him from afar. He's five feet ten inches and solid—thick through the shoulders with a tapered waist. Great calves when he wears shorts. His body looks cut from stone, and I know that because he wears clingy T-shirts. His skin is rich brown, his eyelashes are ridiculously long, fringing eyes so dark they look black from across the room.

"Emma! Hey!" He smiled at me. I gawked like a weirdo, the money clasped in my hand. His jeans looked shabby, like he'd picked them up in a secondhand store, but the current style was to buy them prefaded and riddled with holes, so they could have been brand-new. His sneakers were bright white, matching his polo shirt, and his hair was freshly buzzed, almost down to the scalp. The way he smiled at me called attention to his ridiculous cheekbones and more ridiculous lips and dimples.

Dear God, he has dimples. It's just not fair.

"You ordered pizza, right?" he asked, looking from me to the receipt. In all the weeks we'd ordered pizza, Shawn had never before been our delivery guy.

"Yeah, I… Sorry." I traded him the cash for the boxes. "You're working at Papa Antonio's now?"

"Got the job last week. Cash money is a good deal."

"Cool. Hope you like it." When he tried to make change from my twenties, I waved him off. "Keep the tip."

"Thanks. Nice T-shirt. I loved that movie."

Shawn pointed at my chest before he turned and walked back to the car. For a moment, I pretended he wasn't eyeballing the *Shaun of the Dead* logo and the large, gnashy-toothed zombie on it and instead was transfixed by my charm. And by charm, I mean boobs.

"Thanks!" I called after his back.

He lifted a hand but didn't turn around.

I gazed at the curb long after his car pulled away, ignoring the cold until Nikki waddled out of the house, the foam pedicure thingies still affixed to her feet. "Are you communing with the pizza? We're hungry."

"Shawn Willis," I croaked.

"What about him?"

"He delivered our food."

Nikki giggled and swung an arm around my shoulders, guiding me back into the house. "The Shawn Effect, huh? You should ask him out."

"He likes *Shaun of the Dead*. And no."

"Why not?"

I didn't answer because the truth embarrassed me. I breathed my air, Shawn Willis breathed air from a different stratosphere. Quinn's stratosphere, where thin, pretty people did thin, pretty people things and chubby nerd girls were ignored.

Quinn was a resilient creature. I expected her to mope around the house lamenting the loss of her silver-tipped baby and his donut-y goodness. Instead, she engaged in hard-core retail therapy wherein she outfitted Versace with enough tiny sweaters to last him sixty New England winters. She also wrote Josh Winters off completely. He'd been low-ish on her priority list before, but now he was somewhere around toilet-level.

I only knew the last because she announced it as we followed my mother around the grocery store, dragged there together after a half-day school pickup. We were far enough behind Mom she couldn't hear us, but close enough we could see her Patriots sweatshirt as she pushed the carriage through the aisle.

"I think Josh suspects the thing with his dad. He's been avoiding me, but you know what? He only got me the job because he wanted to do me. Not gonna shed any tears for him." The words were for me but her attention was on her phone.

"Eh. I feel sorry for any kid whose parents divorce. What happened to you sucked, but it's not Josh's fault. I wouldn't wish our situation on anyone," I said.

Quinn's head jerked up, her eyes big like I'd said something completely out there. "You aren't happy at home? I thought you were. Like, our moms love the shit out of you."

"Not really. I mean, they do, but I'm not always happy." I could have mentioned she made me miserable when she did mean and selfish things, or that I missed my dad and that got worse the closer we got to Christmas, or that Karen's way of nonparenting drove me crazy, but that would open Pandora's box and I liked Pandora contained and tidy in her packaging.

Quinn's noticing someone else's feelings for the first time in… forever. That's improvement, right?

"Huh. You never seem down. I kinda hate it here. I miss my old school. My old friends. Dad's house has seven bedrooms. None of this three-bedroom shit. And I miss my dad, too, of course." She glanced back at her phone and managed a smile, though I was pretty sure it wasn't for me or our conversation. She kept talking in my direction anyway. "I wish he hadn't married that bitch. She only wants his money and he only wants her tits, which are totally fake. She says they're not, but

I saw the ridge when she was sunbathing. Of, like, the saline bags? So, yeah. Whatever. She needs to go."

"Oh."

Because that was the only available answer. We'd gone from my feelings to hers. Again.

She ignored me after that, texting to her heart's content, but I didn't care. The conversation made me think about things I didn't like to think about, like my own parents' divorce and the resulting living situation. Grocery shopping became a thing of torture that would never end. When we got home, I helped Mom with the bags while Quinn escaped to her room to avoid manual labor.

"I need your help with the Christmas tree this week," Mom announced. "Karen's leaving for a conference on Tuesday. I wouldn't put one up at all with you girls being older, but your grandmother will have a fit if there's nothing festive in the house. You know how she g— Are you all right?" Mom punctuated the question with a slam, the ham in her hands crashing into the empty sink.

I nearly jumped out of my skin. "Y-yeah. Yeah. I was just thinking about Dad."

"Oh?"

I shrugged. "I probably won't get to see him on Christmas with his flight contract. It's bumming me out."

"Oh, honey." Mom crossed the kitchen to hug me tight, her chin perched on my shoulder. "The holidays are hard. Why don't you go give him a buzz?"

"I will."

"That's my girl." Mom's hand clapped against my butt in an affectionate, football-player-esque slap. I swatted her away and climbed the stairs, reaching into my pocket for my phone as I crossed into my room. I had no idea where in the world Dad was or which important person he might be carting around. If he was midflight, he wouldn't answer, but I wanted to connect if I could.

You there? I typed.

In Dubai, sweetheart. Middle of the night. Everything okay?

The phone was a lead weight in my palm as I figured out how to reply. Yes? No? Christmas sucked? I'd forgotten Dubai was seven or eight hours ahead of me. Telling him I was upset would keep him up asking questions and he probably had to fly tomorrow.

I settled for a simple, I'm okay. I love you and miss you.

You too baby girl. Be home soon. Can't wait to see you.

It wasn't what I'd been looking for. It wasn't *enough*. I crawled into my bed, wrestling with a heap of unpleasant feelings, when Quinn walked, uninvited, into my room. If I'd returned the favor, she would have fired torpedoes at me, but what was good for the goose was definitely NOT good for the gander.

She waved her phone under my nose.

"I want a black-guy rebound." She tapped her cell phone so I had to look at it. I expected any number of things to be on the screen, but a penis—a black man's penis, to be exact—was not on the list. "Shawn Willis. It's all I want for Christmas."

CHAPTER SEVEN

I COULDN'T STAND THAT SHE LIKED HIM.

This is why I don't ask him out, Nikki. Boys like Shawn Willis aren't for girls like me.

"Can you NOT? Not right now," I pleaded.

Quinn glanced from the phone to me before flopping into my computer chair, her cackle evoking images of green-skinned crones looming over cauldrons. "Virgins are so lame. Anyway, I think I'm going to ask him out. He's hot, and it's on my pail list."

I had to process "pail list." At first I thought she meant pale as some awful dig at Shawn's blackness, but then I realized she meant…

"It's bucket list."

You moron.

"You knew what I meant." The click of acrylic nails striking plastic touch screen grated on my last remaining nerve.

She didn't notice. "Are you coming to Melody's party Friday night?"

I groaned. The only reason I knew about the party was because Quinn had mentioned it in passing every day for the past week. It wasn't that she wanted to hang out with her stepsister. No, she wanted a designated driver. I didn't drink a lot. It wasn't because I thought drinking was bad or anything, but the one time I'd had a few wine coolers with Nikki, I'd woken up the next day feeling like a rat had clawed its way out of my skull.

The mistake I'd made was mentioning that fact to Quinn. Ever since, she'd drag me to parties so I could cart around her friends. I probably should have declined the invitations, but the party scene intrigued me. I was the sober scientist and they were the stupid, drunk specimens in my petri dish.

But this time she'd be after Shawn.

"I don't think so," I said, rolling away from her.

Just leave me alone so I can mourn Shawn's loss in private? Please?

"Don't suck, Emilia."

I gritted my teeth. "Not right now, Quinn. Please? I'm not in the mood."

"What? What's wrong?" There was a clatter—her phone against my desktop—and then a hand clapped on my shoulder. French manicured nails, curling over, gripping me.

Wait, is she trying to comfort me?

"Emilia?"

The planets have aligned. She-Thing knows sympathy.

"I really want to go to this party. You're killing me," she continued.

Right. The party.

Priorities, Quinn. Your party over my aching heart.

"I'll do anything. Like, name it," she pleaded. "You can drop me off and leave and then come later to pick me up?"

So you can scoop up Shawn…

"Quinn. I really want to b—"

"Please, Emma? I'm serious—"

"FINE! Just leave, will you? Take a hint!" The hand on my shoulder pulled away, the phone scraped across the desk, the door shut behind her.

From the hall she said, "Cool. Seven o'clock. I'll be in here at six to get you ready. Take a shower beforehand so I can straighten your hair. Oh, and if you're riding the crimson pony, I've got Midol. Let me know."

Riding the crimson po—

My period. Ugh. Go away, Quinn.

By the time her door closed, my lip was trembling. My pulse pounded, my eyes welled with tears. The boy I loved was on her menu—the special of the day. I tried to stop thinking about it, but the more I willed the thoughts away, the brighter they burned, branding themselves on my brain. I was a sobbing mess within minutes. I cried about anything and everything. Dad. My living situation. Shawn and everything he represented. I wanted my mom, but I didn't want to have to go downstairs and get her, so I sniveled into my pillow until my temples throbbed and the only thing I could do to make myself feel better was to sleep it off.

We showed up to the party late, when the festivities were well under way and everyone was already half-drunk. I wore jeans and a pink hooded sweatshirt, Quinn wore a halter top and a skirt so short it could function as a belt. She stopped in the doorway to admire Shawn across the room.

He stood in the kitchen with his friends, Evan and J.T., all three of them sipping from red plastic cups. Quinn jabbed me in the boob, completely ignoring my wince and ensuing self-fondle to massage the ache away.

"He's my Snickers bar. I want to eat him," she whispered.

It took me a minute to make the leap. Snickers were packed with peanuts, so maybe she meant—no. Nope. That's not what she meant. Chocolate. Because black guy. It was racially insensitive Friday in Quinn-ville.

"...I'd leave that out in your great courtship plan," I said. "It's asshole-ish to say."

"Courtship? What are you, eighty? Ugh." Quinn raked her fingers through her strawberry hair before waltzing into the house. When Melody saw her, she let out a squeal that Quinn echoed, and the two of them collided in the middle of the living room, lacing their fingers together and hopping up and down with a hypnotizing double jiggle.

They whispered to each other, their voices drowned by the blasting music. I took that opportunity to find a dark corner and lurk. There were about forty kids there, and while a few smiled my way or waggled their fingers in waves, most ignored me, drawn into the whirling vortex that was my stepsister's small-scale celebrity. She blew kisses and hugged people like she hadn't seen them mere hours ago. A queen among her subjects, granting benediction by not being overly douchy in their general direction at this particular moment.

I glanced at my phone to see what time it was. Half past nine. Our curfew was one, but I gave it a fifty-fifty that we'd make it in by three. Our moms knew it, too; as we left the house, Karen pulled me close and said, "Thank you for watching her," followed by, "I'll handle your mom. You're a peach." She knew what I contended with. Karen understood.

Sort of.

If she totally understood, there was no way she would allow Quinn to climb Shawn Willis. And Quinn was climbing Shawn Willis. It had taken her all of ten minutes to get from the door to Melody and over to The Prize. Shawn didn't seem to mind too much that a gorgeous girl was leaning into his side, looping her arms around his waist, kissing his cheek. He didn't seem to mind when she put a hand into his pocket and bit his ear, either. It wasn't much of a hunt when the prey was completely fine with being devoured.

I tried very hard not to think about it. Thanks to chips, dip and an unending supply of soda, I succeeded. Bonus when Sarah Goldman came to talk to me. We shared a few classes, and she looked as out of place as I felt, so we claimed a love seat and chatted for the better part of the night.

I didn't see Quinn again until after eleven. She and Shawn had disappeared not too long after the pocket-molesting kitchen introduction, tongues and hands doing that marauding thing that made me look away because *Hi, uncomfortable*. She came barreling down the stairs with her high heels in one hand, her phone in the other. Her top was askew, a large purple suck mark blazing at the base of her neck. She whipped her head around, her hair no longer perfectly styled but wild and looking like something had nested in it.

Seeing no one in the room she actually wanted to talk to, she honed in on me, scampering down the last few steps and practically vaulting the coffee table. She waved the phone under my nose like an Apple product offering.

"Look, look!" she said.

I looked. Why I was surprised it was yet another penis, I do not know.

I put up my hand as if warding off a blow, one eye closing, the other scrunched narrow so my world shrank to a slitted window. "Can you stop with the dicks? This is embarrassing for both of us."

"It's perfect!" she exclaimed, loud enough so everyone in the room heard. They crowded around to take a look over her shoulder. Some giggled. Some gasped in disbelief. Then the text messages started happening. Quinn shared the picture with anyone and everyone who'd give her attention, Shawn none the wiser because he hadn't surfaced yet.

I shriveled into the couch. It was so wrong. It was so *exploitative*. That's when my brain reminded me of Mr. Riddell—I'd let a good man down because I'd let Quinn bully me out of speaking up.

Don't do it again, Emma. Be better this time, my brain said. *Don't let fear of Quinn rule your life.*

I steeled my nerves. For better or worse, it was on like Donkey Kong.

CHAPTER EIGHT

SHAWN WAS BUTTONING HIS PANTS WHEN I FOUND HIM. It was distracting, but then, everything about him was distracting, and once again I had to fumble for words, even knowing parts of him had been in parts of Quinn minutes ago. It didn't negate his beauty. It just made it rusty. Less shiny.

Tainted by Quinn.

"She's showing it to everyone. Your…you know."

Shawn jerked up his head, blinking. "What?"

"She's showing your dick to people. Like, texting it. I figured I'd warn you." It came out flat, but I'm not sure how normal anyone would sound telling a not-really-friend that his last hookup was showing off pictures of his pants parts.

"You've got to be shitting me." He shoved past me to run down the stairs. I heard him yelling Quinn's name, I heard her yelling back, and then all hell broke loose.

I have to ride home with her. This was not a flawless plan.

I clung to the idle hope that maybe Shawn wouldn't

tell her how he found out, but no, a minute later Quinn screeched my name at the top of her lungs. Shawn would have been told eventually, with or without me, especially if she'd sent the picture far and wide, but *me* being the one to drop it on her doorstep, *me* telling Shawn so he could handle it on the spot, was unacceptable.

So I did what any brave person in my position would do. I hid in the bathroom behind a locked door and convinced myself not to cry.

Why did I think this was the right way to go?

It wasn't all nobility on my part and I knew it. I was mad at her. Quinn took the daydream that was Shawn Willis and got her stink all over it. Like she did with everything else in my life: my home, my friends, my school. Quinn polluted the world by being Quinn and when she'd taken yet another thing away, I'd latched on to the excuse and gone right to Shawn.

"You fat bitch! You're going to wish you were dead! Do you hear me, Emilia? You're done," she screeched from downstairs.

I couldn't hide in Melody's bathroom forever. I took a deep breath and headed downstairs, fishing for the car keys in my hoodie pocket. The moment my foot hit the living room floor, Quinn rushed at me from the other side of the house. She was red-faced and furious and still frazzled from her tumble with Shawn. Her eyes were wide and red-rimmed, and only got wider and more red-rimmed when she pelted me with one of her shoes, hitting me square in the shoulder.

Holy crap. Manolo Blahnik hurts.

"I'm leaving," I said through gritted teeth.

Quinn let out an unintelligible scream and lunged at me. It was Shawn that put himself between us, getting himself smacked upside the head for his efforts. He grunted, but when she tried to step around him to lash at me, he sidestepped. He never touched her, letting his physical presence bar her from doing whatever it was she wanted to do to me. She pushed him and screamed at him but he never flinched away.

Nor did he ever speak. I took it as my opportunity to leave. I'd parked on the curb, not the driveway, so I could get us out when the time came for us to go home. For me to go home. Singular. There was no way I was putting myself in tight confines with the shoe-throwing lunatic behind me. Quinn's voice followed me into the cold night. I could hear her as I put the key into the ignition and started the engine. I could hear her as I peeled onto the street. Only distance let her to fade to a shrieky, ear-stabby memory.

My hands clamped on the steering wheel, my heart pounded in my chest. I'd done the right thing, maybe not for all the right reasons, but I'd done the right thing. And yet I regretted it. By the time I pulled onto Elm Street, the Christmas lights on the houses had blurred to blobs of blinking color thanks to my tears. By the time I pulled into my garage, I was covered in snot. I snagged a paper napkin from the cup holder in the car and blew my nose, only noticing after the fact that it was a Bouncing Bear napkin.

A near-hysterical giggle escaped my lips.

Why was Quinn so screwed up?

I headed into the house, the cold freezing the boogers inside my nose, and wasn't that a pleasant experience. As I walked into the kitchen, Karen grabbed her purse from the counter, my mother chasing behind her.

"She left her there, that's why," Karen snapped.

"I'm sure there's a reason. Emma doesn't abandon… Hello, Emma."

Both moms whirled my way. My mom bit her bottom lip. Karen eyed me furiously. I had to assume Quinn called and gave her a crap explanation that painted me as the jerk for leaving her at the party, but one look at my face and her anger dissolved. She *knew*. She *knew* it wasn't on me. It was probably far easier to blame me—to believe it might not have been her daughter being the problem child for once, but my misery dashed that hope.

"What did she do?"

I have to tell her. In for a penny, in for a pound.

"She threw a shoe at me," I said. "She got mad and threw a shoe at me. She took a picture of Shawn Willis's dick and showed everyone and I warned him what she was doing so he could stop her. She'll probably try to kill me when she gets home, if fifteen minutes ago is any indication. The only reason she didn't kick my ass was because Shawn got between us."

I swung my gaze to my mother. "You told me to give this a shot. I have. She hates me. I hate her. There's all there is to it."

"Emma," Mom said quietly.

"What? You want to argue this? I could tell you things that'd turn your hair white. I'm actually afraid of her. And no one ever does anything to her when she's a jerk so she's going to keep being like this and I'm going to suffer for it. I'm done."

Karen sucked in a breath like I'd gut punched her. Mom reached for me, but I tossed my keys on the table and double-timed it for the stairs, not wanting to deal with either of them. Nikki was on a date, and Tommy and Laney were at a family Christmas party at Tommy's aunt's house, so I couldn't even call them to tell them what had happened.

I was alone on a Friday and everything was stupid.

Two things happened that night that made the situation palatable. The first was my mother talking to me. It took her twenty minutes to come up, but I'd heard Karen crying, and my mother's job as her partner was to calm her down.

She knocked on my door before poking her head inside. "Can I come in?"

"Are you going to bitch at me for leaving Quinn at the party?"

"Nope. But watch your language, please. I don't want the swearing to become habit."

I motioned her in, pausing my video game so I could give her my full attention. Mom eyed my room—the rumpled sheets, the clothes on the floor, the empty cans of soda lining my desk—but said nothing. She smoothed out the blankets at the foot of my bed and settled in so she was eye to eye with me in my computer chair. Her hands rubbed along her thighs, telegraphing her nervousness.

"Quinn and Karen talked. Quinn asked to move out, so Alan is taking Quinn the rest of the school year. Possibly longer."

My heart skipped a beat.

Quinn gone?

Yes. Please. Please this.

"She's not well," Mom continued. "I'm not making excuses for her, but I sincerely doubt a happy, well-adjusted person would act this way. I know it's frustrating for you. It's frustrating for Karen, too. She wants to do right by Quinn, to show her how loved she is, but it always backfires." Mom leaned forward, peering at me from beneath her dark brows. "Forgive Karen?"

I ran a hand across my brow, the first vestiges of a headache threatening my temples. "Yeah, sure. Whatever. I like Karen. That's never been the problem."

"Well, for what it's worth she's asked Alan to get Quinn into therapy. It's a long time overdue if you ask me."

Last I heard, therapists don't perform exorcisms.

I shrugged. "Hopefully. Does Quinn know yet?"

"Karen's telling her in the car on the way here. She went to pick her up from Melody's."

"Keep her away from me when she gets home," I warned. "Or if you can't, I'll call Nikki and crash over there. I'm not fighting with her and I'm not going to see anyone else get hit for me tonight. Shawn was enough, the poor dude."

Mom looked like she had something important to say, but then she shook her head and stood, her giant sigh making her sound like a deflating balloon. "I'd get anything you need from downstairs and lock your door before Quinn gets back. If she screams, she screams. You have your headphones. We'll figure something out, but try to go easy on Karen. She doesn't deserve the hostility, and I think having to give up her daughter to her assh—to her ex-husband is going to be hard for her."

"I like Karen," I repeated.

It was answer enough. Mom ducked outside.

I took her advice and stocked up on soda and snacks before Quinn's return. Screaming and door-slamming heralded her arrival. I caught only the beginning of it, but that was enough to tell me everything I needed to know.

"Whatever, Mom. I hate all of you!"

Slam.

I turned up the sound on my video game. At some point, there was a loud smack against my door that I guessed was a kick, but I just spiked the volume. The gunfire and dramatic music were far better than anything Quinn Littleton could bring into my life.

It didn't do a whole lot to help my burgeoning headache, but it did do a whole lot to protect my sanity.

CHAPTER NINE

THE SECOND REDEMPTION CAME IN THE FORM OF A midnight text. I didn't recognize the number, and almost ignored it, but curiosity got the better of me as I climbed into bed.

Got your number from Nikki. You ok? —Shawn

Shawn Willis was on my phone hours after he'd sort-of banged my stepsister. The Quinn factor diminished the pleasure some, but not completely, and I squealed inwardly as I messaged him back.

Quinn's freaking out. I'm sorry you're in the middle of this.

Thanks for telling me, he typed. I trusted her and I shouldn't have. You want to talk about it? Tomorrow night, maybe?

Going out with him wouldn't be for any of the reasons I'd

dreamed, but it was still an opportunity to spend time with a guy I'd been ogling forever. The two of us becoming friends would be a silver lining to Quinn's penis-picturey rain cloud.

Love to. Where and when? I messaged.

Johnny O'Mac's at 6? I can pick you up.

Johnny O'Mac's was an Irish-themed pub that failed at Irishing with its scattered shamrocks on the walls and slime-green place mats. The food was only okay and there was a weird funk in the ladies' room, but none of that mattered. Shawn could have been asking me to eat in a Dumpster and I would have said yes. My worry was Quinn. I had no idea when she was supposed to leave for Alan's. If she saw me getting into a car with Shawn, I risked more airborne shoes. Or screaming. Or arson. A scene was inevitable and I didn't want to put anybody through that.

Why don't I meet you there? I don't want Quinn to flip out.

Good call. See you then.

I texted Nikki right away. I hadn't filled her in on the party stuff because I hadn't wanted to unpack my feelings, but talking to Shawn made me think maybe living two doors down from a spewing volcano wasn't so bad after all.

Bad night. Call me when you can.

Two minutes later, my phone rang.

"You okay?"

"I think so? I had a fight with Quinn." I relayed everything, from the depression about Christmas to the picture of Shawn's wang to telling Shawn what Quinn had done. I finished with Quinn possibly moving out and the impending dinner.

Nikki whistled appreciatively. "Damn, and all I wanted to tell you was that I went out with a girl from school and it didn't suck. Like, I might not be the only queer kid at Westvale. You have me beat."

"What? Who?"

"Justice Anderson. I asked her if I could tell you and she said okay as long as you keep it on the down low. She's not totally out yet."

I knew of Justice more than I knew Justice; she was petite with dark brown hair, brown eyes and smears of freckles. We shared half a course load, but didn't talk much beyond study groups. She was a cheerleader, and cheerleaders fell into two camps: Quinn's ilk or the girl jocks. Justice was 100 percent girl jock. She played basketball between fall and spring cheer squads and softball in the summer.

Apparently she also played for Nikki's team.

"Cool! Did you have a good time?"

"Oh, yes. She's got boobs for days. Like, you wouldn't know it, but damn. That girl's rocking a fine pair."

"Nikki!"

"What? You get to talk about Shawn and I can't talk about Justice? How's that fair, homophobe?"

I giggled. It felt good to laugh, like I'd tapped the spigot on a keg and let the pressure out. Like I'd popped the zit that was the Quinn situation. There was still plenty of bad stuff going on, but between Shawn and Nikki, things were looking up.

"It's not a date," I said to Nikki. "Like, he probably wants to explain why he let her take that kind of picture. Nothing he's going to say will matter because I'm convinced that's a stupid thing to do, but at least I get to look at him while he rationalizes it."

Nikki hesitated. "I dunno, Emma. It's not *not* a date, either. He could have ended it with the text or called you or let it drop altogether. I'm not saying to get your hopes up too high, but I'm saying don't close that door before you have to."

She had a point. He could have done a lot of things he didn't do, but he asked me to dinner instead.

"Crap," I whispered, a new worry latching on to my old pile of worries because that's where worry went to roost. "What do I wear?"

Nikki busted out laughing. "You dork. I'll come by to help. But remember, you're the one coming to a lesbian for advice on dating boys. If the school finds that out, they won't let you live it down."

"That's because we go to Moron High," I said.

"See, this is why I love you."

I wasn't a morning person, but the concept of Quinn moving out, regardless of how we got to that point, did a lot for my prenoon disposition. I woke up chipper. Hopeful. *Eager* for that night's dinner with Shawn. No more live-in witch. No more snarly Versace. No more…anything bad.

The lollipop-and-unicorn fantasy evaporated when I saw the black BMW at the curb of my house through my bedroom window.

Alan Littleton.

Alan was Quinn's father. He was also a lawyer, but unlike Karen who I associated with Glinda the Good, Alan evoked images of slithery things. Handsome slithery things, but still—he was everything you saw on TV courtroom dramas when they showed the overly polished defense attorney with his three-thousand-dollar suit, capped smile and rakish good looks lying through his teeth. After Karen and he split, he married a woman a few years older than his daughter, bought that woman a bubblegum-pink convertible that Quinn insisted should have been hers and spent an awful lot of time traveling to tropical places inviting melanoma.

He was also where most of Quinn's problematic personality traits originated. Quinn's manipulative behavior? Alan. Quinn's temper? Alan. Quinn's materialism? Alan. Every single ugly personality trait of the daughter spawned from the father. How Karen lived in a household with both of them for over a decade without becoming an ax murderer, I'd never know.

I donned my royal blue bathrobe with the Tardis logo and dared to venture into the hall. Quinn's door was closed, loud music playing inside. Knowing I wasn't free and clear of her shoving my head into a wood chipper, I sped downstairs. Three steps from the bottom, Alan's voice thundered through the house, loud enough to rattle the pictures on the wall.

"Maybe if you spent more time asking the important questions, she wouldn't be sucking off boys on camera. Drugs happen, Karen. Don't think for a second I'm not taking you back to court to amend the custody agreement. I'm not paying child support to a shitty mother."

Alan was being a jerk. Again. The last time he visited was the weekend of Quinn's birthday when he got her a card congratulating on her sixteenth birthday, which would have been fine if she hadn't been turning seventeen. She'd been pretty upset until he'd offered to take her to Paris over the summer.

Paris fixed a lot of boo-boos.

I rounded the corner. The adults were clustered around the kitchen table, my mother glaring daggers at Alan, Karen with her head in her hands. Alan leaned over her, his skin furiously red against his silver-tipped hair.

"Quinn isn't on drugs," I announced. "That isn't her thing."

Alan had been gearing up for more yelling, but seeing me, he deflated. He ran his hand over his shirt, his fingers worrying the stitched logo of the shark on the chest. "Emma."

"She isn't on drugs," I repeated. "She had to take a pee test to get hired at Bouncing Bear and she passed no problem. She drinks sometimes, yeah, but I know the kids she runs with. Drugs aren't their thing." I looked to my mom to make sure I hadn't misstepped by opening my mouth, but her attention was fixed on Quinn's dad.

Alan cleared his throat. "Thank you, though I don't see how this is any of your business. Maybe you should go upstairs and let the adults talk."

I was more than willing to sequester myself from the douchebaggery for the duration of Alan's stay, but Mom's voice lashed out, as loud as his had been, and infinitely less pleasant, which I didn't think was possible.

"You will *not* tell my daughter what to do in her own home." My mother wedged herself between me and Alan, her finger pointed at his face so she could, if she wanted, jab him in the eyeball. "You wanted to blame drugs for Quinn's behavior, Emma says no drugs. She obviously knows more about your kid than you do. Have some grace or go sit in your car until Quinn's ready. You won't abuse my family in my presence."

"Your family?" Alan tossed his head like an angry horse, the vein in his temple throbbing—*pulse, pulse, pulse*—and wondered what would happen if it actually erupted. Would it be Blood Vesuvius all over my kitchen floor? "I suppose my daughter is the one who suffers here, if you're so protective of *your* family."

I glanced at Karen's huddled form, her frailty a terrible, tangible thing. Normally, Alan's vitriol was met with enough ice to resink the Titanic, but losing Quinn to Alan had worn her to the last nerve. She didn't have it in her to fight.

So I decided I would. "Bullshit. Sorry for cursing, Mom."

Alan's head jerked up; Mom's whipped around. Karen peered at me through the splayed fingers pressed to her face.

I gestured up the stairs. "Quinn's the only kid I know who gets designer clothes for failing report cards. Karen's too nice to her, if that's possible. I'm sure when she moves in with you, she'll be your princess until you or your new wife tell her no. Good luck when that happens, 'cause Quinn doesn't do no. I guess you'll see then who suffers."

The color drained from Alan's face. The reminder that eventually Quinn and her stepmother had to interact—and it wouldn't be good with Quinn's low esteem of the new Mrs. Alan—hit him like a train. Which suggested to me he hadn't done a whole lot of thinking about his invitation to take in his poor, beleaguered daughter beyond "Punish Karen, she sucks forever."

For a lawyer commanding top rates, he sure had cruddy insight.

"I'm going to wait in the car." He didn't wait for a response, instead hustling outside. No one in the kitchen moved an inch until his BMW's engine turned over. For that matter, I'm not sure anyone *breathed* until then.

Karen withered into her seat. "Thank you, Emma. Talking to him can be like talking to a wall. A spiky, nasty wall." She reached for my mother's hand. Mom stroked the backs of her fingers with her thumb before sitting in the chair next to her and pulling her close, Karen's head nestling into her shoulder. "Alan likes to take digs. It shouldn't bother me anymore, but Quinn's a sore subject."

"I understand." And I did. Quinn was a hundred and twenty-five pounds of condensed evil, but she was Karen's hundred and twenty-five pounds of condensed evil. You don't have to like your family members to love them.

"Thanks, Emma," Mom parroted. She rubbed her chin against Karen's hair and smiled at me, her hand sweeping along Karen's spine. "You done good."

I did? Cool.

"Thanks."

I planned to spend the rest of my morning alternating between freaking out about dinner with Shawn and hiding from Quinn, but then the harpy herself appeared, dragging a half dozen pink suitcases behind her. She launched the first down the stairs, damn near taking my head off in the process. I ducked out of the way, the luggage striking the wall and crashing to the floor with a thud two feet to my left.

"I cannot wait to get away from you bitches," Quinn hollered, chucking a second and third suitcase. "This town sucks, this family sucks. I hate it here."

"Quinn." Karen broke away from the kitchen table to approach the stair rail, nearly taking a bag to the face herself. She yelped as it smashed into the bathroom door, cracking open upon impact and raining lacy panties and bras everywhere. "Quinlan! You're going to hurt someone."

"Do you think I care?"

No, I silently thought.

...As did everyone else there, probably.

Karen shook her head, kneeling on the floor to collect her daughter's underwear and stuff them back into the carrier. Quinn's worldly goods kept tumbling down in bags and boxes until I was pretty sure there was no feasible way for the girl herself to navigate the minefield she'd created. She managed it, though, and, once she'd gotten to the foot of the stairs, I stepped clear so she wouldn't mow me over.

She passed by me, never once making eye contact. It seemed she'd *nothinged* me.

I was cool with that.

"Quinn. Please." Karen wasn't quite begging, but it was close enough. "You know I love you. You asked to move back in with your father. Did you want me to fight you on it? I thought you hated it here."

"You picked Fatty, so now you get to keep Fatty. Enjoy your shithole."

If that was supposed to hurt my feelings, it failed, but Karen flinched. My mother's jaw ground, too. I thought she'd lash out with the sharper side of her tongue, but she kept quiet, probably out of deference to Karen's feelings.

I was almost disappointed.

Quinn stormed past all of us to bring her stuff to her father's car. At no point did he help. Karen offered her the bags but Quinn screamed at her to leave them alone. It wasn't a happy kitchen, and when Quinn had the last big suitcase in her hands and was hauling it to the door, it only got less happy.

"I love you. Do you have your EpiPens? Make sure your father sweeps for anything peanut or strawberry," Karen called after her.

Quinn said nothing. She was almost to the car with the last of her stuff when Versace started barking upstairs from her room. She paused only for a second, tilted her head forward and then climbed into the passenger side without him.

"She forgot her dog?" I reminded anyone who might want to do something about it.

"No, no." Karen rubbed her palm across her forehead. "Alan won't let her take him."

Oh.

Dandy.

CHAPTER TEN

"CAN YOU FEED THE DOG? I HAVE TO TAKE CARE OF Karen."

I popped my head up from inside the refrigerator like a prairie dog surveying its domain: my neck extended, my hands curled over before my body. Unlike a prairie dog, I was holding on to a sleeve of crackers and some canned cheese.

"You're serious? That thing hates me."

Mom slapped a paper plate with a ham sandwich down on the counter. "Yes, I'm serious. Listen to her."

Karen sniveled in the other room. She'd been crying off and on since Quinn left, more on than off, which was super awkward because I practically hummed as I walked around my Quinn-free environment. It wasn't that I wanted Karen to hurt, more that I liked being assault free, physically and verbally, and peaceful living sounded really nice.

Extra nice. Like, skip-in-my-step nice.

"Awesome. I lost one bitey beast to gain another."

"Emma! Be nice."

"I am nice! I'm risking a mauling to take care of the dog. Oh, hey. Can I borrow the car later? I'm going out. With a boy. I know that's crazy, but the planets have aligned. Mercury's in retrogade. Cats and dogs are living together. Pigs have learned to fly."

Mom cast me an unfriendly side-eye. "Don't say that about yourself. You're a pretty girl. When will you be home?"

"No clue, but I can text you."

"Do that." She smiled at me before disappearing into the study. I abandoned my cracker lunch to go to the pantry. Quinn usually carried Versace to his dinnertime, cooing while she plated his food. The wormy jerk wriggled in delight in her arms, laving her chin in slimy kisses. I liked my face intact, so I'd slap some foul-smelling canned stuff in front of him and call it a day.

I headed upstairs with a pile of "beef and vegetables" that looked too much like barf for comfort. I knocked on Quinn's door out of habit, and didn't that make me feel weird, like the ghost of Quinn would berate me for approaching.

Inside, it was stripped bare; the closet was empty, the bureau cleaned out with the drawers still open. Knickknacks lingered on the vanity, and a few posters still decorated the walls, but she'd torn down all the pictures on her mirror and the makeup trays were upended. Her pile of pink blankets was rolled up in a wad at the head of the bed, the pillows strewed about the floor.

In the corner, Versace quivered inside his dog bed, the hair along his spine standing on end.

"Easy, Cujo. I'm giving you food." I tiptoed inside. Versace did not "easy" in the slightest. He yapped, all four paws leaving the floor as he hopped in canine fury. I slid the bowl toward him with a sneaker. He quieted as it neared, sniffing it, looking at me, looking at the food. Eventually, he decided hunger was more important than Not-Mommy infringing on his territory. I was more than content to leave him to his meal and his fury, but then I noticed the puppy pee pads in the corner covered with gross.

"Oh, come on." Leaving the dog to languish in his own waste was too terrible, even for me. I cut a wide berth around the feasting murder-pooch and rolled up the pad, depositing it into the garbage. I laid out another, and as I stooped, I caught sight of a picture that had fallen under Quinn's bureau.

Quinn was no more than seven years old, standing in Walt Disney World with her mother and father. She didn't look anything like the girl I knew. The resemblance was there, of course, but this was before the polish: her hair was in braids, her knees dirty, her sneakers extra pink against her white socks. She had a missing tooth in front and a T-shirt with a cartoon character on it. Karen's arm was slung across her shoulders. Alan's hand was behind her back. Their smiles were bright and happy and so very unfamiliar.

This is what makes Quinn so angry. Losing this.

Unbidden thoughts humanizing the terror that stalked my night.

Uncool.

I wasn't sure what to do with the photo. On one hand, it seemed like the type of thing that should go somewhere special. It was a moment from their family past, when things were simpler, or at least looked that way. On the other, Karen was downstairs bemoaning her loss, and wouldn't this make it worse? So I hid it. I don't know why I did, but

I did, in the bottom drawer of Quinn's dresser, and then I closed the other drawers to hide the evidence.

"If you don't hold still, I'm going to rip an eyelash from your head."

Nikki had me pinned to my computer chair so she could pluck my eyebrows. I'd asked her to come over to do my makeup, but she'd given me the full monty, from hair styling to a moisturizing treatment that made my face smell like Fruity Pebbles to ripping excess facial hairs out by the root. She also picked out my outfit: a button-down white shirt over a black tank top, my newest pair of jeans and black sneakers.

"You're lucky I like you. Otherwise I'd kick you in the taco," I growled right before she yanked another hair. I squealed like a pig.

"You're going to look in the mirror and die at how cute you are. *Now. Hold. Still.*" Her palm shoved my forehead into the headrest before those silver tweezers dived for my lip, grabbing on to a hair beneath my nostril and jerking. I yipped and squirmed, wishing she'd spontaneously combust. Or that Versace would avenge me with a flying, yappy-dog attack. Maybe he hated me less after feeding him. Probably not, but one could hope.

Nikki pulled back to assess her work, her red lips spreading into a Joker-esque grin. "Awesome. The swelling will go down in a minute or two."

She rooted through the pile of cosmetics littering my desk to procure a hand mirror, shoving it in my face. I stared. I hadn't been this done up since the fall formal with Tommy.

Had I attempted to do it myself, I would have looked like I was wearing battle paints.

Which would be oddly appropriate if Shawn proved to be a serial killer, which was one of the reasons I'd contrived for him asking me out in the first place.

"It looks good," I said.

"Never doubt me, Padawan."

"Yeah, yeah." I watched her gather up her stuff into its various plastic pouches. "I'm still not sure I should go. With Quinn gone it feels… I dunno. Karen's all weepy."

"We've been over this. If he's being friendly, you make a friend. If he's not, he's a hot guy you went to dinner with. And whatever about Quinn. She's done ruining your life for a while. Enjoy yourself. Karen will chill when she remembers she doesn't have to deal with her kid's crap anymore." She walked over to smooth my shirt, sweep my hair over my shoulder, and poke at my still-swollen brows. They felt like they'd been mauled by fire ants, but the ache abated minute by minute. Until she prodded them, that is, and I swatted her away.

"Stop that."

She fussed at me before reaching for my glasses on top of the bureau. "You look awesome. Here."

I slid them up my nose, not letting them touch my eyelashes in case the mascara wasn't dry. "I'm nervous," I confessed, my stomach caterwauling for food. I'd skipped lunch figuring I'd fit better in my jeans without it. Bad plan. I couldn't tell if my guts were screeching Swamp Thing's mating call because I was hungry or if it was the tightness of my pants.

"I know, but you'll have fun. Do you think I'd tell you to

go if I didn't believe that?" Nikki stuffed her makeup into her over-the-shoulder bag, leaving a mauve lipstick on my vanity. "Okay! I've got my cell. Let me know if you two head for J.T.'s and I'll meet you there. Have fun. Wear a condom!"

"Condom? Jesus, Nikki. Cart before the hors— Wait. What's at J.T.'s?"

J.T. was a classmate I'd known since kindergarten. I vaguely recalled him being one of the paste-and-Play-Doh-eaters. Oh, and he got to use the cool green-handled lefty scissors while I used the plain righty ones in Mrs. Cullen's class. That was over ten years ago and the extent of our association. "There's another party tonight. Justice invited me. I'm sure I could score you an invite if you and Shawn break early. I think Laney and Tommy are going."

"Oh. Okay, maybe. I'll ask Mom."

"Do it. I'll talk to you later. I gotta get ready myself!" She double-timed it for the door. A minute later, I heard the questionably dulcet tones of her radio over the squeal of angry tires.

I headed downstairs. Quinn was always busy right up until go time—on the phone, on social media, painting her nails. Dates weren't a big deal. Sitting by the front window waiting for quarter of to come because I didn't want to get to the restaurant too early made me feel desperate. I pulled out my cell, thinking of texting Tommy, but I was pretty sure he didn't want to listen to me freak out about a boy.

Laney? No, she's at work.

So I waited. And fretted. And waited and fretted some more before climbing into Mom's car and driving to the plaza parking lot in front of Johnny O'Mac's. I checked my reflection in the rearview mirror. I still looked nice, put together for me anyway, but my glasses took up a third of my face. I was so scared of nerding too hard at Shawn, I shoved them into the glove box. The world blurred, no longer distinct shapes but color smears across a canvas. I blinked through it, wishing I'd taken my optometrist up on her offer to prescribe me contact lenses six months ago. I'd declined because I didn't trust myself not to poke out my own eyes trying to put them in.

I fumbled my way out of the car, my vision slowly returning, which was good because two cars down, Shawn Willis climbed out of his car and it would have been strange for me not to recognize my own dinner date. Tight jeans, a pair of black sneakers, a button-down black shirt. He looked prettier than I did, and I immediately regretted everything about coming.

I have no business being here. I'm going to say all the wrong things and do all the wrong stuff and...why is he so hot? This isn't even fair.

Panic was the only thing that kept me cemented to the parking lot pavement. Well, panic and the knowledge that if I ran, I'd not be able to live with myself. I clutched the car door wishing I could vanish, but then Shawn lifted a hand, a bright smile spreading across his dark face.

"Emma. Hey, looking good."

Oh, God.

Oh, God. Oh, God. Oh, God.

CHAPTER ELEVEN

"GOTTA ADMIT, I'M DISAPPOINTED," SHAWN SAID, SLIP-ping his hands into his pockets.

We're not even in the restaurant yet.

"Why? Is— Hi, by the way."

He grinned. "I was hoping you'd wear one of your T-shirts. I like the Loki one, but here you are all fancy. You look great, but now I feel underdressed."

I wasn't wearing Loki the night he delivered pizza. That was Shaun of the Dead. *Which means he's noticed my T-shirts before.*

Holy crap.

"Oh."

I had no idea what to say.

Think, Emma. Think.

"I'm like Superman," I blurted. Shawn looked confused, and I swallowed past the lump in my throat to explain. "Or Clark Kent. You know how we all know he's Superman, but you slap some glasses on him and he goes incognito? I'm the opposite of that. Take off my glasses, there's a girl underneath." I looked down at myself, in particular at the round assets I harnessed with a lacy sling every morning. "I think."

Shawn laughed, a rich, warm sound that made me want to rub against him like a kitten. Since that would probably get me maced or slapped with a restraining order, I laughed, too, mine a bit too braying donkey for comfort.

He ran a hand down the front of his shirt, stretching the material taut and flashing sculpted physique in the process. "Let's get you some food, Superman. J.T.'s having some folks over later if you want to come with. Should be a good time."

Better. We're doing better.

"Yeah, that's... Sure. Nikki mentioned the party. Wild weekend with Melody's last night and J.T.'s tonight, huh?"

"Christmas parties for the win. Parents are away a lot this time of year." He fell into step beside me to walk to the restaurant, rushing out to open the door as we approached the entry. I thanked him and slid inside. A healthy crew of people surrounded the bar, their heads tilted back to watch the hockey game, but the dinner tables were sparse. We were seated immediately.

Napkin on lap, elbows off the table, look normal.

I was failing so hard at normal. Shawn is so fun to look at, and he was right across from me doing his pretty thing, and every time I tried to say something my tongue went to taffy. Fortunately, he was ready to steer the conversation ship into port on his own, which was good, because I was as useless as boobs on a duck.

"So, the elephant in the room, eh?"

I almost asked what elephant but then I remembered my stepsister's existence.

"Quinn? What about her?"

Shawn picked up his menu, his eyes scanning the selections, probably so he didn't have to look me in the eye, which was understandable considering we were about to discuss something that, by the flush in his cheeks, embarrassed him. "I've never done anything like that. But we'd had a few drinks and she… You probably don't want to hear this about your sister. I know some dudes wouldn't think anything of it, but my mother raised me better than that." He tilted the menu down to peer at me. "Did you see my dick?"

One moment, I was contemplating onion rings. The next I was contemplating nothing at all because *he really just asked that.* I'd never looked so hard at cheeseburger choices in my life. "A little?"

Not the right thing to say, Emma.

"It wasn't a little di— She shoved her phone in my face so I couldn't not see it, so it was a flash of— Yes." I sucked in a breath. "I did. I'm sorry. I looked away right away."

"Dude, don't apologize to me. You did me a solid. I don't know many people who'd take on Quinn like that but you did and that was… Yeah. That was something." He reached over to brush his fingers against the back of my hand. I stared at his beautiful skin against my pasty nastiness. "You're cool, Emma. I like cool."

"I am *not* cool." I hid behind my menu, focusing on the tacky green lettering at the top of the page because the other lettering was hard to read without my glasses. "I'm a huge dork."

Shawn shook his head before motioning the waitress over to take our drink order. "Nah, you're cool. You're not going to convince me otherwise, so stop trying."

I stopped trying. We ordered or meals and settled into some cursory chitchat until our food was delivered ten minutes later. His question of "What are you into?"—dropped right before I dug into a pile of vinegar-slathered fries—terrified me.

Everything dorky. No, seriously, everything.

It was going so well, too.

Shawn either didn't notice my distress or was polite enough to pretend he didn't. He bit into his French Dip sandwich so ferociously, it was like he was trying to murder the cow right there at the table.

"I dunno. Stuff?" I said, feeling lame.

"Like what stuff?"

I didn't want to tell the truth. Comic books. Reading. Anime. Video games. Basically, if you took a thing society attributed to nerd culture, I liked it, and I didn't want to flaunt my raging dorkiness in front of someone who was, according to my high school, a cool kid.

"Action movies?" It was actually comic book movies, but action sounded more mainstream so that made it safer.

"Cool. I like martial arts movies. The Marvel movies. Comedies like *Shaun of the Dead?* Oh, and check this. Musicals. Like, the old ones? Love those. Ginger Rogers, Fred Astaire."

I had a French fry in hand, but hearing that this buff guy liked musicals, I boggled at him from across the table. It didn't compute. He was so…masculine.

He's gay. That's why he asked me out to dinner. Friend date all the way.

It was a terrible leap to make, but my moms had a lot of queer friends, and a lot of the guys liked old musicals. And

Barbra Streisand. And Judy Garland. My brain betrayed me by buying into the stereotype before I could tell it not to.

I couldn't say as much, so I sputtered out like an old car engine. Shawn didn't seem to mind, wiping ketchup off his chin and checking his shirt for splotches. "I know what you're thinking. I like chicks. I just like dancing, too. I figured if I told you, you'd loosen up."

I nodded, but loosening up? Oh, no. No, no, no. I tried, but that wasn't happening, especially when he leaned over the table to close the gap between us, very nearly squashing his chest into the other half of his sandwich. He tapped the back of my hand again, the brush of his fingers making me squirm.

"I also take dance lessons," he confided in a conspirator's whisper. "Ballet. Jazz. You want dirt, there's dirt. I'm a dude ballerina. Everyone thinks it's the football, but I got this body doing pirouettes."

He grinned from ear to ear and that was it—I burst into laughter. I relaxed into my seat, cramming a fry into my mouth and smiling around it.

"Seriously? I can't dance at all," I said between mouthfuls. "Like, I'm awful at it."

"Everyone says that. It takes practice."

I took a deep breath and, for the first time, dared to look him straight in the eye. Contrary to any previously held beliefs, it was not like looking straight into the sun. Yes, I melted, but it was a pleasant melting: less ice cream on summer pavement, more chocolate chips inside of warm cookies. "I appreciate what you're doing. Joking. I take a while to relax, I guess."

He went back to his dinner, ordering a second round of

sodas for us when the waitress stopped by. "Good. Now are you going to tell me anything about yourself?"

"Okay. Well, uh. I like to read. I'll read anything. I love *Doctor Who*—"

"Is that the guy with the magical screwdriver?" He interjected. "The English guy."

"It's future tech, not magical, but...yes."

I considered launching into a time-crafted theory about The Doctor's chosen implement, but Shawn cut me off with, "I always meant to watch that but I never got around to it. I'll have to check it out. You ever watch *Supernatural*? I've been catching up on that. Up to season four now. It's pretty good for a show about white boy tears."

Common ground. We had it in Sam and Dean Winchester.

Hallelujah!

"Yeah," I said. "I love that show."

I smiled at him. He smiled back.

The ice was officially broken.

CHAPTER TWELVE

"QUINN MOVED BACK IN WITH HER DAD," I TOLD SHAWN.

The party started at seven. We'd talked until after eight at the restaurant and then followed it up with ice cream from a local roadside dairy. The cows that squirted out our treats grazed near our picnic table, filling the air with a distinctly barnyard *odeur.* I glanced at Shawn, a gob of ice cream falling from the top of my cone to splash the back of my hand.

"Because of the picture thing?" He looked surprised.

"Less that and more because of our fight, I think. We'd both had enough, and she likes her dad better than her mom. He lives richer. Quinn's an expensive commodity."

"She's something all right. I have no idea what I was thinking." He swiped at my dollop with his napkin. I cast him a grateful smile and licked my cone. So very vanilla and boring—like me, Quinn would say.

Shawn plunked the remains of his ice cream into a paper cup before pulling out his phone to check the time. It had to be getting late. The farm workers were rounding up the livestock to return them to the barn. The lights in the parking lot flicked on behind us.

"You don't have to keep defending yourself," I said. "Quinn could be persuasive when the mood took her."

"Too bad she didn't put that to any good use." His fingers flew over his phone, firing off a text to J.T. "It's almost nine. Sounds like things are in full swing if we want to head over."

"Sure." I took a last bite of ice cream and threw away the remains. Shawn called my name, and I paused. He reached for me, his thumb brushing the corner of my lip to sweep off a crumble of cone. His smile softened when he touched me, his eyes narrowing enough that I could tell he was considering something.

Me. Considering me.

At that moment, I would have given all the pennies in the world to know his thoughts.

"You're really pretty." His hand dropped away and he went back to his phone. He didn't look at me, but the soft smile lingered.

I took those last few steps toward the trash bin. "I'm okay for a fat chick."

I winced the moment I said it. Nikki whacked me whenever I did the self-deprecation thing, but it had become a coping mechanism—a way to ward off Quinn's meanness. If I devalued the digs before they were said, they couldn't hurt as much, right?

It's like Shawn knew that's why I did it. He looked up, but the smile was gone and in its place was a flat grimace. "It must have been rough living with Quinn. You're nice and smart and a lot of things she wasn't."

"Thanks, but I'd counter with she was a lot of things I'm not, too."

"That just means people can stand you for more than five minutes." He went quiet a second before adding, "Hey, do you want to come over tomorrow night? I know it's a Sunday, but maybe we can watch some TV, get some Chinese. My parents are heading up to Maine to visit my older brother, so we'll have the house to ourselves."

I froze. That wasn't what I'd been expecting, but then, the whole night had been a surprise. The fact that we had anything in common astonished me. While I wasn't a dancer and he wasn't quite as steeped in nerd culture as me, we shared interests. We listened to the same music; we both wanted to go to New York colleges. Through mutual fits of giggles, we confessed our shameful adoration of Disney movies.

"You mean like a date?" I asked.

And wished I hadn't, because once again, I felt like a dumbass, but I had to be sure this wasn't a pity gesture on his part. My pride wouldn't stand for a "take out Emma because her stepsister was a hag" overture.

Shawn laughed. "Yeah, a date. Unless you're not into it. I'd understand. The Quinn thing *was* only yesterday." He motioned at our cars parked side by side in the lot. We walked to them together, our shoes crunching through the gravel all the way.

"I'd like that," I said before I could screw up any further. "To hang out tomorrow."

He smiled and climbed into his car. "Cool. So would I."

It took me a while to get comfortable with Shawn one-on-one. A party with a zillion kids? Wasn't going to happen.

There were cars everywhere. On the lawn, along the curb, parked half in the woods, half out. It was good J.T. lived on a dead-end street or the cops would have been all over the place. It was conspicuous.

Shawn could tell I was nervous. At least, that's the reason I gave for him touching the small of my back when I climbed from my car. I nearly jumped out of my skin, but I swallowed it down before I made a fool of myself. I even managed to sidle in against him. My hip bumped his and he winked at me.

It was adorable.

We approached the front door. My stomach clenched, a gooey, tingly happiness oozing through me. I rarely prayed, but standing beside Shawn on J.T.'s front step, I begged God to not make this some huge joke. I didn't want to get lured into a comfortable place with Shawn only to find out that Quinn had been right all along. That fat, brainy girls didn't deserve Shawn-caliber guys.

She'd told me that once, after she found out I'd dated Tommy.

"You should have stayed with him," she'd said.

"Excuse me?"

"You won't do better than him. I mean, it's cute to aim high, but you'll just be disappointed."

"Are you kidding me?"

"Huh?" She'd tilted her head like a confused dog. "No? Hotties stick with hotties. Nerds with nerds. Jocks with jocks. It's just how it is."

"You just suggested high school dating apartheid!"

"Apart what?"

The notion that the prettiest stars glimmered among

other stars while the rest of us languished below, pining for what we could never have, had infuriated me. I was so angry, I made gobbledygook noises, sounding an awful lot like a backed-up garbage disposal.

Quinn had cocked her head to the side again. "What? It takes work to look how I look. It's less genetics than you think. It's investing in your appearance. Fat girls can get skinny. Ugly girls can wear makeup. You get me. You want to date better than Tommy, you need to up your game."

"The superficial shouldn't matter more than the person inside," I'd snarled. "We shouldn't segregate ourselves based on whatever label you apply to us."

"You think boys think like that? Let's test it. We'll line up my boyfriends next to your single boyfriend and see who's right."

I'd been furious. But the worst part about that conversation was, months later, out with Shawn, her screwed-up philosophy came back to haunt me.

Shawn can date girls like Quinn. He can do better than me.

Stop. Don't let it have brain real estate. It'll ruin everything.

Breathe, Emma. Breathe.

J.T. opened his front door to usher us inside. With his black hair and green eyes, he was pretty cute despite half a face of acne scars and his hat on backward.

"Come in, come in. Sup, man." He clapped Shawn on the back in a bro hug before eyeballing me, an indiscernible look on his face. "Emma. Cool. Glad you could make it."

"Thanks."

Kids were everywhere inside. Clustered in corners, leaning over the stair rail, on the back patio, entering and leaving the bathroom. A hundred bodies swarmed. I knew most of them, had grown up with most of them because people born in Westvale had a depressing tendency to die in Westvale when they were old and gray, but that didn't make it less daunting. It only *added* to the strain. They'd already deemed me ignorable. Why would they acknowledge me now?

J.T. motioned at the kitchen. "Drinks are back there. Got a keg out back and the hard stuff on the counter. Help yourself. Bathroom down the hall to the left and one upstairs."

"Thanks," I managed, very much a stranger in a strange land. Shawn must have sensed my fight-or-flight because he grabbed my hand. The moment we touched, it felt like everyone in the room turned to stare. I expected snickering and whispering, but it wasn't like that at all. It was more like people were seeing me for the first time. I was no one until I'd become Shawn Willis's date.

It was a somewhat depressing realization.

"You thirsty?" Shawn asked. We maneuvered our way through the throng toward the kitchen. He could have let me go, but he didn't. That he wanted to touch me at all made me feel better. Seeing Nikki would have helped my panic, too, but she was nowhere to be found.

"Yeah, sure."

"What do you w— Oh, hey, man. Sup?" Shawn stopped short in the hall before the kitchen. I bumped into his back, jabbing my nose into his shoulder and cringing. He was tall enough I had to poke my head around his elbow to see who'd crossed his path.

Oh, goody. Josh Winters.

CHAPTER THIRTEEN

QUINN'S A PAIN IN MY BUTT EVEN WHEN SHE'S NOT *physically here anymore.*

"Is the whore here?"

Josh's greeting left a lot to be desired. Sure, he was hurt and angry, but that didn't mean I was keen on him blaming his father's stank dong on the underage girl he'd banged.

"If you mean Quinn, no," I said.

"Good. Fuck her. Oh, wait. Willis already did."

Shawn stiffened in front of me, his grip on my hand tightening. "Not cool, man. How many drinks you had?"

"Enough."

"Why don't you go chill out somewhere before you say something you'll regret?"

It wasn't a threat, but it wasn't exactly friendly, either. Josh took it in stride, too inebriated to care as he staggered to the living room. I watched the back of his head until it disappeared behind a wall of tittering, gossiping girls.

Shawn turned to look at me, obviously annoyed. "Sorry. I didn't bang her, though."

"You've got nothing to apologize for, and that's none of my business even if you did."

Shawn ran his hand over his fade. "Want to find a place to sit?"

"Sure."

Shawn guided me through the throng, shouting out hellos to the people who greeted him along the way. I didn't have that problem, mostly because my friends either weren't there yet or had snuck off to party parts unknown. Everyone else looked at me like something that belonged on an Area 51 autopsy table.

We were almost to the front door when a lavender blob swooped in from my right. Melody loomed over me in her pale purple blouse and perfectly winged eyeliner. I stared at her. She stared back. Melody was pretty and popular with her short curly black hair, big brown eyes and a tan so golden chicken nuggets were jealous. She was also the notorious party puker; every time I'd played Quinn's designated driver, Melody was the one who had me pull over six times on the way home so she could paint people's front yards with Strawberry Boones–scented vomit.

"What are you doing here?" Her attention swung over to Shawn. "Nice, Shawn. Nice. The next day? You replaced Quinn with this?"

This. I was a thing. Less than human.

Great. First Josh, now Melody. I want to go home now, kthnxbai.

"Yeah, I upgraded. The last model had a serious case of Asshole."

Melody's eyes narrowed like a sun-soaking cat.

Maybe if I stay very still and very quiet, the predator won't sense the scared rabbit in her midst.

"If you think this means everything's fine now, you're wrong. She's my best friend and she's gone because of your stupid cow."

Under normal circumstances, I'd have ducked my head and scurried off to get out of the blast zone, hoping that this, too, would pass, but something about the dig got my temper going. Quinn's insults from Melody's mouth sent me from zero to homicidally irate in two point five seconds.

"If you believe Quinn left because I told Shawn she showed his dick to people, you're pretty dumb. Quinn hated Westvale, hated the school and thought everyone here sucked. So maybe, for once, you can use that pulpy meat inside your skull to think instead of letting your face hole flap with stupid."

Silence. Not just from her, who looked like I'd slapped her, but from everyone around us. Inside, outside—it didn't matter. The party was put on hold because Emma MacLaren had finally lost it on a mean girl.

Just not the mean girl they would have expected.

Oops.

"Damn. You got told," Shawn snickered. It was some kind of social cue; kids whistled, kids laughed and the noise picked up again, everyone talking about Emma and Melody and *what went down*. Except I wasn't exactly sure what had gone down? I'd won? Not that anyone ever won during fights, but I wasn't quivering or sobbing, so that had to be better than the alternative.

Right?

"Whatever." Melody took off, her black curls bouncing around her ears as she disappeared in much the same way Josh had, the crowd swallowing her into its gullet.

Well. This sucks.

"I need some fresh air." I broke away from Shawn to escape, brushing past a few classmates and their dates on the way out. I'd made the leap from ignorable girl on Shawn's arm to party-ruiner, or if not ruiner, gossip fodder, and I wasn't sure what that meant for me in the long run. I considered going home, or finding Nikki, Tommy or Laney and talking to them, but I wasn't sure which way was up. I plopped down on the brick front step, focusing my anger on the hapless garden gnome peeking up at me from a nest of ground cover. I toppled it, but found no satisfaction in its facedown, mulchy demise. My head dropped into my hands, my eyes pinched close so I wouldn't cry for reasons I couldn't altogether understand.

After all, I didn't want mascara tracks all over my face.

It wasn't Shawn that found me five minutes later sitting on J.T.'s step, bullying a lawn gnome, but Nikki. I didn't see her coming, but I definitely heard her when she bellowed across the yard, "What's wrong?" She trotted my way from the street, her purse in one hand, a plastic bag full of glass bottles in the other. Her hair was no longer a purple unicorn party but a blue so bright it hurt my retinas to behold. It was also much shorter than it had been a few hours ago. She'd cut it down to a crazy, spiked buzz-cut thing. Her makeup was rocker glam—all silvers and blacks and cobalt blues. Her black leather coat had gray fur along the collar and sleeves.

She looked badass.

"Do I need to shank a bitch? Shawn texted me saying you were upset. I blew a red light to get here."

"He did? That's cool of him, but no shanking needed, thanks anyw—" I didn't finish the thought because the side door slammed and out came Shawn holding two cups of beer.

"You looked like you could use a drink. Hey, Nikki. Looking good." Shawn sat beside me, offering me a foamy cup of what smelled like a mix of gasoline and pee. I sipped anyway and immediately regretted it. Beer was an acquired taste, they said. I hoped I'd acquire it soon or this would be an even more unpleasant evening than the "sabotaging myself in front of my graduating class" scenario.

"Sup. So what happened again?" Nikki glanced at us and then at the house, her brow knitting. "Someone being a douche?"

"Melody was being Melody, but Emma slapped her down. I don't think she'll mess with her again." Shawn tipped his glass to me and then his hand came out to rest on my knee, giving it a gentle squeeze. It felt nice. I eased closer to him, the outside of my thigh touching his. He didn't pull back. I tried one of those subtle, over-the-shoulder glances to see if he was grossed out.

He caught me looking. Because *he* was looking *at me*.

I looked down into my beer cup. Because *I'm* a coward.

"I… Yeah. I wasn't looking to make anyone look bad. Melody took a shot and I told her off. It's much ado about nothing."

Nikki moved her bag from one shoulder to the other. Glass clinked against glass. I had the distinct impression Nikki wasn't gracing the party with a bunch of apple juice.

"I'm going to bring this stuff inside. It's getting heavy. Anyone want anything?"

I waved her off and she disappeared around the corner. Shawn and I sat side by side on the step, him drinking his beer, me thinking about drinking mine. As a kid, if I didn't like something, I'd pinch my nose so I couldn't taste the nasty whatever. I didn't think that'd be quite as okay in high school.

"Should I even go back inside later? They probably think I'm a killjoy." I swirled the beer around, took a deep breath and guzzled half of it in one go. I didn't like it, but enough of it and maybe I could forget about my life. Maybe my senses would be dulled enough that it wouldn't taste like liquid dog farts.

"I think they were impressed. Melody's normally not out-bitched." Shawn winced and tilted his head my way, his nose crinkling. I wanted to run my finger over the mini-ridges between his eyes. "Not saying you're a bitch, but you did put her in her place."

"No offense taken," I said.

We fell into an amicable silence. Inside the house, the stereo blared a dance track Quinn had often played on Repeat in her room. It made me squirrelly. Here I was, at a party she should be at, with a guy that had been with her less than twenty-four hours ago.

"I'm out of my element, I think. Like this… I know you guys have parties all the time. I'm usually not invited, which is okay," I quickly added, not wanting him to think I was feeling sorry for myself even if sometimes, it hurt to not be included. "But I feel like I'm playing make-believe in Quinn's world. It's weird." I drained the cup and crushed it in my fist.

White fissures riddled the plastic. I traced the paths with my thumb, my eyes straying to the felled gnome.

It looks pathetic all facedown.

"It's not weird. It's new and new stuff can be scary. Tonight does feel different than other parties but I think that's because there's no one dancing on the dining room table half-naked yet. Quinn had a few signature moves."

Shawn slid the cup from my grasp, eyeballing the damage. "This cup has been structurally compromised. Be back with a refill."

"Okay."

The moment he turned the corner, I righted the gnome—silly Sunday school and its Catholic guilt. I was brushing the mulch off his ugly gnome face, digging the dirt out from the creases near his too-big eyeballs, when Nikki came back. Except she wasn't alone. She dragged Tommy and Laney behind her, both of them sporting swollen lips and glassy expressions, Tommy wearing more of Laney's black lipstick than Laney did.

"Stop kidnapping our classmates," I said to Nikki. "It's a felony."

"I dragged these two here with me. They were dry humping in the car the whole way. I figure they need air before they die."

Laney rolled her eyes and reached into her purse for her lipstick. Seeing Tommy's sad condition, she offered him a tissue before touching up her own makeup. "Says the girl who will be doing the same as soon as she sees Justice."

"Well, yeah. I'm a poster child for hypocrisy." Nikki plopped down on the lawn, fanning her fancy coat out behind her. "People are being dicks to Emma. I figured we should do that thing where we act like friends."

"Huh, what happened?" Tommy snagged the mirror from Laney and cleaned up his face.

"Eh. Melody took me to task about Quinn. I've gone from being on one shitlist to another."

Tommy frowned. "Quinn sucks. So glad you don't have to deal with her anymore."

"Don't say her name three times or she might appear," Laney murmured.

"I know, I know. She's the worst, but I'm fine, I swear." I gazed off into the night, beer taste souring my mouth. The woods to my side rustled with the wind, and I had the thought that this was how horror stories started—a secluded spot, drunk teenagers and a murder yeti hungering for man flesh. "These woods are wicked. I think I saw a movie like this once."

Shawn chose that moment to return with our drinks, and didn't the hinge on the door squeal in that awful, haunted house way. I flinched. Shawn paused to eye me, then the door, his red Solo cups held aloft. "Everything cool?"

"Worrying about murder yetis. Thanks for the drink."

If he thought that was strange to say, he didn't indicate as much. Maybe our hours together had inoculated him to my flavor of Out There.

He settled in beside me, offering me my drink and looping his arm around my back, his fingers resting comfortably on my hip. I slumped into his side, my cheek pressed to his shoulder. It felt good. Fuzzy, but good. The fuzziness might have been the beer, but I wasn't going to think about it because thinking was hard.

"I appreciate you all coming to check on me, but really, go party. I'm okay." I didn't say that so I could get Shawn alone, but Nikki's smirk indicated she thought that's what I was getting at. She winked at me, I snorted at her and she got up to nudge Tommy and Laney back toward the house.

"See you guys soon? Maybe?"

"Go inside, Nikki."

"'Kay!"

Laney waggled her fingers at me. Tommy followed suit, oblivious as usual.

The door closed shut behind them and I was left on the stoop, drinking beer and canoodling with *Shawn. Freaking. Willis.* My *quasi-complicated dream come true.*

CHAPTER FOURTEEN

I SIPPED MY FOURTH FROTHY DEATH-IN-A-CUP, GRATEFUL I'd stopped tasting it after the second glass. It was that gross. Shawn and I hadn't done a whole lot of talking, but there'd been no making out or fondling, either. It was two people sitting side by side, hand in hand, companionably in the darkness, a party blazing on behind us that neither of us cared about. It was good. I was comfortable. Everything was going swimmingly.

Until my phone rang.

I glanced at the screen.

Mom.

"Oh, crap."

I'd forgotten to call her and it was past eleven. I stood up, wobbling like a sapling bending with the breeze. Shawn reached out to steady me, his hands settling on my hips. I managed a grateful smile as I tottered through the grass to get away from the ridiculously loud house. "Gotta take this. Be right back."

"Everything okay?"

"Yeah. It's my mom."

I headed toward the trees at the edge of the property, considerably less concerned about a murder yeti than I had been earlier. Kids horsed around nearby, laughing and squawking and tackling one another, but I was pretty sure I was far enough away they wouldn't interfere too much with my call.

"Hello?" I shouted into the phone.

"Where the hell are you?" came the angry maternal rebuttal.

"Hey. I'm so sorry. I totally… I meant to call. We went to dinner and then he brought me to a friend's house. I forgot."

There was a long pause on the other side of the phone. Mom's silences never boded well for me; they were the precursors to shouting and flames bursting from the sides of her face. It didn't help that one of my classmates started screeching a string of F-bombs that would have made a trucker blush.

Alarm bells bellowed in my beer-addled brain.

"Since when do you go out for the night and not tell me where you're going? And how long you're going to be gone? And who you're with? I've been sitting with a crying Karen all night expecting to hear from you."

"S…sorry. I'm sorry. I've been out of it this week. I… Nikki is here and I… Yeah. Sorry," I stammered. I wanted to say something better, but the beer had robbed me of my capacity for speech. Worse, Mom knew it.

"Have you been drinking?"

Lie. No, wait. Don't lie. It always makes it worse.

"A bit," I admitted. "But I'm not driving."

"You're damned right you aren't. Where are you?"

"J.T.'s house. At the end of Lou Gehrig Drive. But, Mom,

seriously, I'm okay. I'm sorry I didn't say anything. It escaped my mind. Shawn Willis asked me out."

"I don't care if Channing Tatum asked you out. I'm coming to get you. Be ready in fifteen minutes."

"Wait! Mom, please." If she collected me like a toddler from a playdate, I'd look stupid in front of my classmates. I did a great job of doing that without any help. I sucked in a breath, willing myself not to cry. "Please don't. I can get a ride home from someone sober, but if you come get me in front of all these people, they'll make fun of me forever. I'm already having trouble. The first thing that happened when I got here was Melody blamed me for running Quinn off. I'll come home, just please let me…please."

More silence from Mom. I didn't actually expect her to relent, but then she growled much like Versace. "Fine. But if your driver's not sober, I will kick your ass so hard you'll have butt coming out of your mouth. Bring my keys home. We'll get the car tomorrow. I'm not pleased, Emma. This is not okay."

"I know. I'm sorry."

Mom hung up. I slipped the phone into my pocket and closed my eyes, willing the drunk away. I was going home to an ugly conversation and a grounding. The happy buzz that allowed me to float along carefree had become an enemy.

My shoulders slumped, my head hung low. Shawn rose from the stoop to join me by the tree line. He walked fine, not at all sloppy, less affected by the beer than I was. "Anything I can do?"

"My mother's pissed. It's my fault. I forgot to call her. I was so… You know, dinner. So I forgot and she's mad. I gotta find Nikki to see if she can drive me home. I'm sorry."

Shawn pulled me in for a hug, his hand sweeping along my spine. I was rigid for the first few seconds, but then I sagged into that firm body, accepting the comfort, enjoying the smell of his cologne. Spicy, musky. It was something good. None of that Axe Body Spray crap.

"No apologies, Superman. If you can't come out tomorrow night, we'll do it when you can. I'm not going anywhere."

I was so happy he said that, I bit back a snivel.

"You're cool."

"Nah, you are. We've been over this." He pulled back to peer at me, smiling, and then he kissed me, right there in J.T.'s yard. My stomach fluttered, my pulse pounded in my ears. Shawn's fingers swept through my hair, his head tilted to match his mouth to mine. Lips and teeth and a hint of tongue and every worry I had disappeared.

So did the oxygen.

It was everything I'd ever dreamed of. My fingers bunched in his shirt, my legs squeezed together. I was so high I could have taken flight. The boy I'd adored since he'd moved to Westvale in sixth grade was kissing me, and in a weird way, I had to thank Quinn for it. If she hadn't pulled her Terrible Person routine, he never would have talked to me, or stroked my back, or nuzzled at my hairline before pulling back.

"Go find Nikki. I'd drive you myself, but I've had a few."

"Yeah. Right. Nikki."

Brain. Brain work now. Brain work times? Please?

I staggered through J.T.'s side door, squinting against the light. Shawn was a solid presence behind me, his fingers resting on my waist to keep me from falling over myself. It was hot inside despite the windows being open and the

December air blowing through. Body heat from dancing. Body heat from drinking. Body heat from kids making out in corners. The place reeked of booze and pot smoke, and I pressed through the crowd, stepping over the people littering the floor in giggling heaps.

Nikki's hair made it a short search. It was a bright blue beacon in a sea of brunettes and blonds. She was on the steps, a shadow-lurking body writhing against another huddled form. Because her partner was a girl, she had an audience. A half dozen boys watched and grinned. Mike Allegrini was a little too happy to be watching, if his pants were any indication. When I kicked him in the ankle on the way to the stairs, it was only half-accidental.

"Put your junk away," I snapped, stepping over a groping couple who turned out to be the field hockey captain and the vice president of the senior class. Oops.

"Shut your face," Mike snarled, but he had the good grace to hobble off, his hand hovering over his crotch like that would call attention *away* from his man problem.

Ascending the stairs proved a Herculean feat—Shawn had to relinquish his hold so I could maneuver. I slithered behind a nearly screwing couple, wedged myself between two dudes talking and holding beers, and vaulted a pair of whispering girls to get to the top of the steps. Nikki was doing a damn good job of assaulting Justice Anderson, and Justice seemed more than happy to assault right back. Her hands roamed through Nikki's hair. Nikki's hands explored under her shirt. Every kiss was accompanied by the muffled groan of *they are totally gonna do it.*

Had I not been drunk, it probably would have been a

whole lot more daunting to interrupt them. Fortunately or unfortunately, beer dulled a lot of my good sense. I never would have talked to Mike like that sober, either, but…well, I guess I felt like I didn't have a lot to lose after respective Quinn, Josh and Melody confrontations.

I tapped Nikki on the shoulder. She lifted her head. Her bottom lip was shiny with saliva—hers or Justice's or both, I didn't want to know. Justice's freckled face was rosy, a big suck mark forming along the underside of her jaw. Both of them gazed at me, Nikki not all that friendly-like, Justice's pupils so big they covered her irises.

"You're jealous, aren't you? That's why you're here," Nikki said. "If you wait your turn, I should be free in an hour."

I forced a sheepish smile.

"Have you been drinking?"

"No." Nikki looked smug, her fingers twining in Justice's bra straps and tugging, forcing Justice's body to collide with her own. "I've been busy."

Justice swatted her away, but she was smiling.

I cringed. "Cool, but you are going to hate the hell out of me in a second because I need a HUGE favor."

Nikki was surprisingly cool about driving me home. Every time I apologized—and I apologized a lot standing on the stairwell—she waved me off with a, "You'd do it for me."

She was right, I would, but I still appreciated it.

"The trouble is me getting my car out. I was jammed in. Bear with. I gotta find out who parked behind me."

I said my good-night to Justice and slinked off with Shawn to wait outside. Explaining to my classmates that I had to leave early because my mommy was mad was shrivel-up-and-die-worthy. It was better to make a mysterious exit and let them wonder.

"You're sure you're okay?" Shawn asked when we were alone, both of us loitering on the curb beside J.T.'s driveway. "I know I've asked before, but you look upset."

"I still feel stupid," I admitted. I wanted to say something smarter, but the beer and my brain were fighting and the beer had thus far claimed flawless victory. I was dizzy and woozy, my stomach displeased with my life choices. The prospect of getting home and facing an enraged Mom Machine didn't help.

I pulled out my phone to text Laney and Tommy and tell them Nikki was taking me home. My thumbs were the drunkest part of me, and I thanked God for spell-check or that message would have looked like a love letter from Cthulhu. "I'm worrying and being dumb."

"Family comes first. I totally get that." He reached up to tuck a lock of hair behind my ear. I wanted to hug him for being that nice. Actually, I wanted to jump him and kiss him again until I turned blue in the face, but that probably would have been a bad idea. Nikki wouldn't ever let me live it down despite her own tongue Olympics in the stairwell.

"Family comes first until your mom drops a bomb on you," I said. "Or, you know, Quinn's your family. There are days I want to feed her to an alligator."

Shawn smirked. "Touché."

The house door slammed. Nikki reappeared, a kid I didn't know on her heels.

"Van driver—found."

I nodded at the kid. “Thanks for moving your car.”

He grunted at me.

“Okay, well, thanks again for tonight. It was fun,” Shawn said.

“It was, and I’ll let you know about tomorrow night. Thanks, Shawn.” I smiled at him right before he leaned in to kiss my cheek. Another waft of that cologne, the softness of his lips against my skin, and then he was gone, retreating back to J.T.’s house to rejoin the party I had sort-of-but-not-really attended.

“Oh, he’s into you,” Nikki whispered low, her arm wrapping around my waist to guide me to her car. “How amazing is that?”

“I don’t know.” Her dark brows lifted so tall, they kissed the fringe of her blue bangs. I rushed to explain. “I like him, but he was with Quinn yesterday. I keep feeling like this is too good to be true, and after what happened…I don’t know. It’s too fast. It’s…something. I don’t know. I’m drunk.”

“Oh, honey.” Nikki tousled my hair like I was a kid half her age before shoving me into the passenger side of her car. “That was just a blow job. The way he looked at you tonight? That’s butter. It’s good. Trust me.”

When I continued to look dubious, she leaned in to press an obnoxious kiss to my forehead. “*Trust me.*”

CHAPTER FIFTEEN

"KAREN MIGHT PUT UP WITH THAT CRAP, BUT I WON'T," Mom said, rounding out a ten-minute rant at the kitchen table in which she informed me that no call was bad on a regular night, but on a night when Karen was torn up over her kid leaving and Mom was trying to take care of her, I was Westvale's very own Genghis Khan. She didn't quite say the last part, but she insinuated that I was a satanic piece of crap. Okay, she was just really, really mad, but I was upset and drunk and she made me feel like dirt. Mom didn't lose her temper often, but when she did, it was all fissures in the earth and dinosaur-killing meteors.

"I said I'm sorry. I meant it. I got…flust… I got all…" I took a deep breath to collect myself. "I screwed up."

"Keep your voice down. Karen's in bed. Yes, you did. And I don't know why you think I'd be fine with you getting drunk at seventeen, but I'm not, so let's talk about underage drinking, shall we?"

I burst into sobs. It took me by surprise, but once the

floodgates were opened, there was no turning back. Being in trouble, leaving the party, being yelled at while I was tipsy—it was too much. I got ugly blubbery, where my mascara ran all over my cheeks and left me looking like a drenched clown. "I'm sorry. Shawn asked me out and I've liked him for a long time and Nikki said it would be good for me to go so I said okay and didn't think. I wanted to fit in. Quinn always does and I… For once. That's all. For once."

I expected Mom to keep yelling, especially when her lips pursed together so tightly the corners turned white. A worry line bisected her brow, a deep V that looked like it had been stamped there. But instead of shouting, Mom fizzled out. The anger was gone, replaced by something that looked a lot like defeat.

"Quinn was rough on you, I know."

"No, you don't know, Mom, that's the thing. You suspect, but you don't know, because she never pulled most of her stuff in front of you. Some, but not all." I used the sleeve of my shirt to dash at my cheeks. The fabric came away with makeup smears. "The kids at school treated her like gold even though they hated her. She pulled the thing with the camera and…I don't know. The only good thing to come out of this week is Quinn leaving. Or, well, Shawn Willis asking me to hang out. That was cool, too. He wanted to apologize to me and thank me for telling him what Quinn was doing. He's a great guy who made a bad choice."

Mom got up from the table to go to the fridge, pulling out the milk. Two glasses and some Hershey's syrup, and a minute later, we were both blessed with giant vats of chocolaty goodness. "We all know Quinn has some issues. We're hoping Alan has better luck getting her help. She didn't want ours. As for this Shawn kid…well, if you tell me he's a good kid, I'll believe you, but right now I'm operating under the assumption that he's an idiot."

"So's he. He's embarrassed." I guzzled my milk, surprised it didn't rebel the moment it collided with the other gross stuff I'd put in my stomach that night. "He's a ballet dancer, and a good student. He asked me to hang out tomorrow. I'd like to go if I'm not grounded."

I was prepared for Mom to say no, if not because of the no-call thing, because of the drunk thing, and if not because of that, because Shawn was the same guy to have his wang posted all over the internet the day before. Instead, she peered at me, clearly assessing, her fingers drumming on the table. "You get one body. Respect it. I don't mean… I get that kids do things." Mom flushed, her attention dropping from my face to her glass like looking at me was too difficult. "You need to remember the risks. Staying healthy, that's respecting yourself. You're on the pill, but that won't protect you from disease. If he's been with a lot of girls…"

Okay, so this didn't go exactly how I planned.

"We're not there yet, Mom. Geez. I've gone out with him once."

"All it takes is once, so be good to yourself. Condoms. Don't do anything you'll regret the next day. As for tomorrow, if you tell me where you are, and when you'll be home, you can go, but be smart. I don't know much about this Shawn guy, but don't get caught up with an asshole. I loved your father but he was an asshole, and the case of gonorrhea he gave me opened my eyes too late to that fact. Learn from my mistakes."

Did she…

Yeah, she did. She went there.

"Mom! Gross!"

"Well, I'm sorry! But these are the realities. As far as the drinking goes, I know kids do that, and I'd rather you be honest with me if you do it. I don't condone it, but I'm also... Always have a designated driver. I know you've been the designated driver, but if it's you, worst-case scenario, call me. I'll come get you. I'll be pissy, but I'll come get you."

"I will. And Shawn...it'll be cool, Mom. I promise. I'll watch out."

I finished my milk and stood from the kitchen chair, desperate to get away from Mom's sharing mood.

Gonorrhea. Things to not want to think about the next time you talk to your dad for one thousand, Alex.

The booze haze made a quick exit feel much, much too difficult. I wavered on my feet, sweaty, uncomfortable and nauseated. Mom offered her hand to me. I slid my fingers through hers and she hauled me close to help me up the stairs.

I texted Nikki, telling her to call me the next day so I could fill her in on my domestic drama. By the time she answered, she was either really drunk or...there was no or. She was really drunk.

LOL boobs was the reply.

The mighty lesbian had spread her wings and taken flight yet again.

I sprawled out in bed, a killer beer headache pounding behind my eyes. The lights were out, the blankets soft, but I couldn't sleep thanks to Versace whining in Quinn's room. There was a light on, but apparently that wasn't good enough. Maybe he was lonely or maybe he caught on to Karen's misery and was riding the wave. They said animals sensed things. Maybe inside of that tiny, ugly head of his, he understood that Quinn wouldn't be coming back.

I tried to ignore the whimpers by putting a pillow over my head. Immediate guilt. The animal didn't understand why he was alone at a ridiculous hour of the night. But what was I supposed to do? He hated me. I could throw the ball and he'd probably attempt to remove my throwing arm instead of fetching. I could walk him around the neighborhood but that'd put my lower half in peril.

He let loose with another whine.

"Aww, c'mon!"

I flipped back the covers and clambered toward Quinn's room. Versace was in his bed, agitated. There was a miniscule growl and a hop at my appearance, his ears standing on end before he did the strangest thing.

He wagged.

"I must be really drunk."

He did it again.

It wasn't the first time I'd seen him wag. He wagged at Quinn all the time, but he actually wagged *at me* before sitting in his bed, his head cocked to the side.

"Okay, I can't pat you, so what do you want?"

Versace tilted the other way. The staring contest began and the dog eventually won because I have no willpower whatsoever. I sat on the floor. I didn't make any movements because I didn't trust him not to come at me, but he never made a move beyond settling into his bed and peering. When I stood up to go a few minutes later, he sat up with me. Two steps and he wailed. This was heartrending stuff, or would have been if I didn't hate the dog. I propped open Quinn's door, put up the baby gate at the top of the stairs and swept my arm behind me.

"There you go, Sparkles. All yours."

The freedom must have been enough. The whining stopped, and ten minutes later, the world's snarliest Chihuahua trotted into my room to fall asleep in a pile of dirty laundry.

CHAPTER SIXTEEN

MY BUZZING CELL PHONE WOKE ME THE NEXT MORNING. I slapped the end table for my glasses before remembering I left them in the glove compartment of Mom's car. A glance at my alarm clock told me it was a blurry ten.

I thought it'd be a text from Nikki, but I wasn't that lucky. I squinted to bring the letters into focus and then wished I'd remained ignorant and blind.

IF U THINK I DON'T KNOW I DO U UGLY WHORE

I WILL RUIN U I DON'T EVEN HAVE TO BE THEYRE

There are moments you want to keep your parents out of your business because everything is less complicated that way. Then there are moments you hide behind them like fleshy walls. I opted for the walls; Mom said she understood what Quinn was like. A pair of poorly spelled threats might help her "understand" better.

I put my feet down on the floor, doing a cursory sweep for Chihuahua of Doom. He'd vacated for greener pastures, which meant my toes were safe. Out the door, down the hall, the stairs and into the kitchen. Moms were seated there, my mother clipping coupons, Karen staring at her laptop, the screen reflected in the reading glasses perched on her slim nose.

"Hey, sweetheart." Karen stretched out an arm to lug me in close, her face pressing into my ribs as she hugged me. "How's the head this morning? The beer biting back?"

"It's fine. Sorry if that doesn't teach me the anti-drinking lesson you were hoping for."

Karen sniggered. Mom stuck her tongue out and went back to her coupons.

"Not to ruin the morning, but I figured I'd let you guys know that Quinn's threatening me. Not sure what she'll do, but she's really good at being unpleasant when she puts her mind to it."

I dropped the cell onto the table, text messages up, and waddled my way to the cabinet for a Pop-Tart.

Mom sighed. Karen groaned.

"Why now?" Karen asked.

"Because the guy she 'photographed'—" I paused to do finger air quotes "—took me out on a date last night. Apparently that's an affront to all things Quinn."

"She can't really do anyth—" Karen started to speak, but my mom cut her off. Sharply.

"Call her and tell her to cut it out." My head whipped around, my mouth hanging open so far a pterodactyl could have used my tongue as a landing pad. Karen looked just as surprised; the parenting had never crossed streams before, Mom biting her tongue whenever Karen indulged one of Quinn's fits, Karen looking away when Mom had to do her occasional yelly thing at me. Something had changed.

Oh, Gonorrhea conversation, you unsung hero.

"I...well. I don't know what I can do is all. She doesn't listen to me."

"So make her. Your kid is bullying mine," Mom insisted. "Talk to Alan. Do something. Quinn's not going to run our house when she doesn't live in it anymore."

Karen's cheeks flushed and she looked down at her laptop. Her head jerked in an abrupt nod, but she wouldn't meet my gaze or Mom's. "I'll call after this PowerPoint."

"Good."

Mom motioned at me and craned her neck toward the driveway. "Get dressed and we'll go get the car. Homework is done?"

"I'll finish today. It's not a lot."

"Good, because you have chores to do before you go anywhere tonight, and it's a school night, so plan to be in by ten."

Mom's expression was flinty. I wasn't grounded per se, but I also wasn't going to get off the hook too easy. I knew enough to keep my mouth shut, finishing my breakfast and returning upstairs to destink myself. I was ready to go in fifteen minutes. When I reemerged, in my jeans and a Star Wars T-shirt that had seen better days, Karen was elsewhere and Mom was making her way to Karen's car. I joined her. Neither one of us spoke much on the way to J.T.'s. I considered asking her why she'd gone after Karen like that, but I wasn't sure it was any of my business, either.

We arrived a little after noon. There was still a whole

bunch of cars on J.T.'s sidewalk, including Nikki's. Apparently everyone had crashed instead of driving drunk, which was somewhat reassuring on the Darwinism front.

"Is that Nicole's car?"

"Yes. She must have stayed overnight." I unbuckled my seat belt and put my hand out for the keys. Mom dropped them into my palm. "I'm going to go check on her before I come home. I haven't heard from her since last night. I want to make sure she's okay."

Mom nodded. "Don't linger. You've got things to do if you want to go out tonight. Do you need anything at the grocery store? I'm stopping there before heading home."

"I won't screw around, and no, nothing. Thanks."

"You're welcome. See you in a bit."

I climbed from the car and Mom drove away. The first thing I noticed approaching J.T.'s house was that the garden gnome faced the wrong direction, a result of my drunken fumbling from the night before. I adjusted it again before knocking on the door. There were groans inside, and some quiet chatter, and then J.T. was there, in front of me, covered in hickeys and wearing the same clothes I'd seen him in the night before.

"Hey. Sorry to bother you guys, but is Nikki here?"

He stared at me incredulously, slow blinks, like I'd been unveiled as the villain in a Scooby-Doo episode.

"Emma?"

"Yeah?"

"Emma!" I heard a nameless boy call from inside the house. "Let her in. I want to talk to her."

This was immediately followed by the snickering of a half dozen other boys, the effect not unlike a pack of hyenas.

Uh-oh.

"Is she here or what?" I demanded.

J.T. ran his hand through his hair, resulting in a cowlick that stood up from his head at a ninety degree angle. "Yeah, upstairs. I think she was still passed out."

He motioned me in. Kids sprawled through the living room, as limp as dishrags, some of them lifting their heads to greet the newcomer and—seeing it was me—smiling, scowling, or sneering.

Josh grinned at me from his perch on the couch, a passed-out Melody sprawled across his legs. A foul-smelling bucket rested beside her head like she and the Boones had done their usual projectile-vomit thing.

"Hershey! You got plans on Friday? I heard we have a common interest. Plus I figure you owe me after what Quinn did." He punctuated the last with a lewd gesture of one finger pumping in and out of the closed fist of his other hand.

The hairs on the back of my neck stood on end.

Hershey? Is this because Shawn's black?

Does he think we slept together? Maybe Shawn left when I did and they assume…

I took the steps two at a time to get away from the leering crowd. I opened every door down a long hallway that smelled of cigarette smoke and stale cologne, searching for my best friend. J.T.'s house was bigger than it looked from the outside, and it took me six rooms to find the correct pile of teenagers. I recognized the spooning girls immediately thanks to Nikki's dye job; her naked front lined Justice's naked back, Justice's brown hair twined around her upper arm.

They looked peaceful and totally at odds with the rest of

the house. Seeing their chests rise and fall indicating *no, not at all dead*, I turned to leave, but Nikki's sleep-drenched voice stopped me in the doorway.

"Hey. You okay?" Her voice was low to keep from waking Justice.

"Yeah!" I averted my gaze when she sat up, the blankets falling and exposing her upper half.

I had no idea she had those pierced.

"My mom told me my dad gave her gonorrhea last night, so you know, that was awesome," I said to the wall.

"Wait, what?"

"You heard me. It was a weird night. She was pretty pissed at me and then gonorrhea happened. Anyway, I gotta go. I wanted to make sure everything was cool." I motioned vaguely in the direction of the driveway. "Came back for my car and saw yours still here. I would have driven you home if you'd needed it."

Nikki tugged on her shirt from last night and stretched. "If I'd needed it, I'd still be drunk. That's not my vice, chickie." She waggled her eyebrows and rolled her head in Justice's direction.

"Right. Sex goddess. You had a good night. I'll head on home."

Nikki swept her fingers over Justice's shiny hair, a smile playing around her mouth. "It was an awesome night. Is Shawn here?"

"No clue," I said. "But everyone's treating me weird and Quinn threatened to ruin me this morning, so I think something's up. Like, Josh asked what I was doing Friday night. That's not at all suspicious."

Nikki's smile evaporated. She slithered out of bed and

reached for her pants, hopping around on one foot to pull them on. I'd always envisioned leather pants being so tight you'd need a spatula to take them off. I never realized you'd need a crane to put them on, too. There was a flash of bare butt before she pulled up her zipper and brushed past me to go downstairs.

"Nikki?" I called after her.

"Wait here."

Something stirred in the bed behind me. Or, well, someone. Justice. She's not a thing. She's actually pretty cool.

"Hey. Good morning, Emma. Are you good?" Justice stretched, fortunately not exposing a second pair of bare boobs before I'd had my coffee. "Did you have fun last night?"

"I don't know? Yes? Maybe?"

I looked from Justice to back toward the empty hallway. I could hear Nikki talking to people downstairs, and then I heard a very loud, very irritable "For fuck's sake," which was followed by stomping up the steps and a slap to the wall.

"You're all idiots!" she bellowed before reappearing to collect her stuff from the guest bedroom floor. "Yeah, I'm getting out of this hellhole. Do you want a ride home, Justice?"

"What's going on?" I demanded. Each of Nikki's abrupt, annoyed gestures birthed another coil of dread in my stomach.

"It's Quinn," Nikki said between clenched teeth. "She told Melody the only reason Shawn would go out with someone like you after someone like her is because you're dirty."

"Dirty?" I sniffed my armpits to make sure I didn't have on *eau du nasty*. Seeing it, Nikki smacked my elbow, probably a fair bit harder than she intended. I winced.

"Not like that. Like you'd do stuff Quinn won't do." Nikki shrugged into her faux fur jacket and spun to look at me. "She told them you were into butt stuff."

"Butt stuff?"

I didn't get it.

And then I did.

Hershey.

CHAPTER SEVENTEEN

LEAVING J.T.'S WAS A BLUR. THERE WERE CATCALLS, and laughter, and Nikki swearing at a lot of people on her way out the door, but I didn't stick around to see how bad it could get. I was too embarrassed. People probably didn't believe what Quinn said, but if it was funny enough or mean enough, kids didn't need to actually believe something to use it to bludgeon their peers.

Me. Emma MacLaren.

Hershey MacLaren.

I drove home mad, which was probably as bad as driving home drunk as I could barely see the stop signs and traffic lights even with my glasses on. I parked on the left of the driveway, leaving the right open for Mom when she got back. I had every intention of busting into my kitchen and going straight to Karen with fiery declarations and hellfire, but as I stormed up the driveway, I heard Karen shout into her phone. A glimpse at her profile showed me a red face and trembling shoulders.

I hesitated on the front step. I didn't want to barge in on what was supposed to be a family moment. Not a happy family moment, but a family moment all the same. Sure, standing outside was voyeuristic, but what else was I supposed to do, sit in the car and pretend I didn't live there?

"Please calm down. I'm not askin— No, of course I don't love her more than you and I'm not taking sides! But you're… Quinlan."

There was a pause. Karen sucked in a breath, her head dropping into her hand. "Quinn, please. Listen to me. You're making life hard for everyone. Yes, I know you're upset, and I'm sorry for it, bu… Quinn. She's not a bad kid, you… Quinn? Hello, Quinn? Are you there?"

She dropped the phone to the table and rubbed her eyes with the heels of her palms.

How do you win against that?

How?

It defused some of my anger. Not all, but enough that I managed to walk into the house and not scream profanities about Karen's sucktastic offspring. When the door clattered shut behind me, Karen lifted her face to look at me, her misery palpable.

"I'm sorry. I'm trying."

"I know." The desire to tell her about the butt thing was overwhelming, but it wouldn't change anything. Quinn would still ignore her. Quinn would go on punishing her for the divorce and maybe her sexuality and definitely her relationship to me. Quinn was the terrible constant in the equation of our family.

At least the lack of proximity meant the screaming wasn't in person any longer.

But she doesn't need to be here to ruin me, remember?

"I'm going up to do my homework," I muttered.

"Oh, Emma." Karen snatched my hand before I could go. Her fingers were cold, icy, as she laced them around mine. "You're an awesome kid. You don't deserve this. I was—am—a crappy mom. I have no idea what to do with Quinn. I'll keep trying, though. Maybe I can ask her doctor or… I don't know."

She didn't know, but I did. Quinn was too old to fix. She was set in her ways, her methods of home-turf terrorism tried-and-true. If she could outlast us—and she could definitely outlast us—she'd win. Karen would end up buying peace, if not for herself, for the rest of us. The pattern would never end.

"Hey, just think, one day she'll be in college!" I said, trying for cheerful when all I wanted to do was take a cheese grater to my face.

Karen stroked over the back of my hand before reluctantly letting go. "No, I don't think so. Not with her grades. It's awful to say, and I don't mean to… Quinn's only real hope is finding a husband or someone willing to take care of her in spite of her temperament." She managed a bark of dry laughter and stood from the table, slipping her phone into her back pocket. "Otherwise she's going to be my and Alan's problem for a very, very long time, and I can't… I can't." She lifted miserable eyes my way. "I can't, Emma."

The dirty pictures started showing up in my text messages as I finished my homework. I didn't know the phone numbers sending them, but they were all local, so I had to assume in Quinn's pursuit of making me look bad, she'd handed out my contact information because *why not.*

It was a thorough slandering through and through.

I'd deleted the sixth piece of pornography in an hour from my messages when Shawn's number blinked on the screen, not with pictures of butts, which was really appreciated, but with a real live call.

He's probably canceling plans. Or, maybe not, but with how the day's going…

"Hey," I said.

"I heard what she did. I'm telling everyone it's bullshit, but…yeah. She's unreal. Why's she so mad all the time?"

I could have tried to explain, but what did I really know? I was guessing based on hearsay and a picture I found of Disney World from ten years ago. Armchair analyzing the pretty disaster in my life was about as much fun as making out with a Cuisinart.

"I don't know. I don't really care, either."

"That's fair." Shawn cleared his throat. "You still coming over tonight?"

"Yeah, I should be. If I have to get pictures of asses off my phone every ten minutes, it's nothing personal. I don't want to have to explain them to my mom if she sees them."

"Ugh. Yeah." Shawn sighed. "I'm… I feel like this is my fault in a way. I'm really, really sorry. Like, you have no idea."

"I don't blame you."

And I didn't. He'd accepted what he thought was a strings-free blow job, the girl had decided to do something crappy in the aftermath. He'd underestimated how hard Hurricane Quinn could hit.

"You're too nice. What time do you want me to pick you up?"

I glanced at the clock. It was three thirty. I figured an hour or so of chores and I'd need another shower. "Five? I have to be home by ten. School night."

"That's doable. Text me the addy."

We hung up, me sending him my address before going downstairs and checking in with my mom. She was in the living room alone, watching some antiques show on PBS. Karen was tucked away in her office. That wasn't typical. They weren't joined at the hip or anything, but they tended to spend weekends together because Karen's job could make her work late during the week, so shared time off was a commodity.

And yet.

I bet they're fighting over the Quinn thing.

If they break up because she's that much of a dysfunctional pain in the ass…

It was a leap, but one I didn't like to make all the same. For all that I didn't like the Quinn baggage, I couldn't stomach the thought of losing Karen. Not for me or my mom.

Uncomfortable. The line of thinking made me *so uncomfortable.*

"What did you want me to do around here?" I asked. Mom rattled off a list, and I ran around like crazy getting everything done as quickly as possible. I was pretty impressed with my overall performance: chores, a shower, dressed and ready to go within an hour and a half. I'd just pulled on a hoodie when Shawn's car pulled into the driveway. I didn't have time to do makeup, or worry about the shirt I was wearing, or straighten my hair, but I did manage to swipe a tube of lipstick from the bathroom on my way downstairs. My glasses went into the front pouch of the sweatshirt.

"Be home by ten," I called to my mom as I trotted out to meet Shawn. Mom sat up on the couch, craning her neck so she could eyeball my date through the front window. I would have been happy to introduce her to him on another night, but with only five hours to hang out with him, I wasn't wasting any time.

Shawn was halfway out of his car when I vaulted into his passenger side.

He smiled, his eyebrows high on his forehead.

"Ready to go, huh?"

"You have no idea."

I glanced up. Mom stood in the bay window, her hands in her pockets, her dark hair collected in a twisted lump on her left shoulder. Shawn waved to her and she waved back. That was a good sign. No shots fired over the hull.

"You got your pretty from your mama," Shawn said before leaning over to press a kiss to my cheek. Despite an incredibly crappy day, I smiled.

"Thanks."

"I only speak the truth. Did you get contacts? I haven't seen you in your glasses. I miss them."

"Oh. Uh."

Now I feel like an idiot. He's going to like me or he's not.

Wear your glasses and grow some girl balls, Emma.

"They're in my sweatshirt. I forgot… Yeah," I lied. I retrieved them from the pouch and slipped them up my nose, the world shifting into focus once again.

Shawn pulled out of the driveway. "How are you holding up? About the…you know. *Thing*? I feel worse than ever that I touched her. Like, she's hot, but I had no idea it'd get this crazy. That's some toxic shit right there."

"*Toxic* is a good word for her," I murmured, thinking back to Karen's abortion of a phone call from earlier. "And I'm okay for now, but I'm not looking forward to school tomorrow. Or the day after that. Or the day after that. I walked into J.T.'s this morning to check on Nikki and Josh asked me what I was doing Friday night before calling me Hershey. Swell guy."

Shawn's brow crinkled with disgust. "He can be a huge toolbag sometimes, and I know he's got a rage-on for Quinn. I'll talk to him. See if I can't convince him to back off. But you know what? That's tomorrow's problem. We've got tonight to hang out. I'll cook us some dinner, we'll watch a movie. It'll be good, yeah?"

I cast his perfect profile a grateful smile.

"Thanks, Shawn. You're the best."

"Nah, sweet thing. That's you."

He reached for my hand and squeezed it. I squeezed back. It was good.

CHAPTER EIGHTEEN

SHAWN SAID HE'D COOK AND BROKE OUT A BOX OF MAC and cheese. With its hysterical orange color, I wasn't sure it could really be classified as food. Also, cooking generally required more than boiling water for twenty minutes and adding a chemical cheese packet. What Shawn did was more accurately called *assembling.* But I was so grateful to be at his house instead of mine, with him instead of people who weren't him, he could have poured milk on cereal and I would have called him Emeril.

"Not gourmet, but it's better than pizza." Shawn smirked. "Don't get me wrong, pizza's good, but when you work for a pizza place it's the last thing in the world you want to eat."

"It's all good. Thank you," I said.

Shawn and I headed for the living room. A squishy couch, TV trays and a few bottles of soda made for the perfect TV setup, and I snuggled into a cushion with my bowl of orange nasty. Shawn fired up *Supernatural.* It wasn't an overly gross episode, which was nice, because you never knew when the show would go from swoony hot men to slither monsters chewing on toddlers.

"Did you tell your mom about the Quinn thing?" he asked during a quieter part.

"I told her Quinn threatened me. My mom told Karen—that's Quinn's mom—to handle it, but I know there's nothing Karen can do. Quinn hangs up or screams louder or… It's pointless. The best I can hope for is the rumor to die down quickly."

"It will. There's a new drama every week. Sorry this is your week. I'll help however I can, though." Shawn pulled my feet into his lap. We sat that way for the rest of the episode, him occasionally rubbing my legs. It helped me forget my awful, chocolaty nickname.

A little while later, Shawn collected our dirty dishes. That left me alone with fourteen mystery text messages, three of which were pictures of uncomfortable-looking insertions. Quinn also blew up my phone with a wall of vitriol, but I refused to read it, blocking her and sending it to the trash where it belonged. When Shawn came back to the room, he tsked and plucked the phone from my grasp, tossing it to the other side of the couch.

"They don't matter, babe."

Babe? Cool.

The TV went off and he turned the radio on. "So you said something about not being able to dance."

"Y…yesssss?" I watched him move the coffee table away from the couch with not a little fear. "That wasn't a challenge, you realize. We can go on pretending that I never said it."

"C'mere." He grinned.

"I'm going to step on you."

"So? C'mere." He held his arms open in invitation. To unsuspecting eyes, it looked like a hug, but I knew the evil that lurked in that facade. "Trust me."

"Fiiiiine." I closed the distance between us. He adjusted my hands, one on his shoulder, the other clasped in his fingers. His free hand rested on my hip, and he proceeded to give me The Idiot's Guide to Basic Waltz in his living room. It wasn't nearly as hard as I expected, and a few times, I forgot it was a lesson at all, my head dropping to his shoulder as we spun gently through the living room.

"This is good," he said into my hair.

"It's baller," was my oh-so-genteel reply, which was met with a giggle.

Over the next few hours, he showed me a few other, simple dances. I likened it to teaching chemistry to a monkey, but Shawn valiantly disagreed, repeating the dances until I only stepped on him every fourth step instead of every other. Everything went to hell when he upped the ante. Jazz squares confused me so much, I tripped over the reclining chair, and when I spun to my left instead of my right with a basic twirl, both of us fell onto the couch laughing until our stomachs hurt.

Which turned into kissing, because laughing and kissing go together like peanut butter and jelly.

There were makeouts. Legendary makeouts. Makeouts like I'd never seen before, his lips on mine, teasing, with enough tongue to feel good without all the slobber. It was amazing. We snuggled up together, content to be two bodies in a space only big enough for one, me sprawled over him. His hand caressed my hair, from my bangs all the way down over my shoulders to the ends.

"Who knew you could like Clark Kent?" I said quietly, my fingers tracing over the whorls on his button-up shirt. The silvery thread pattern allowed me to explore great swaths of his oh-so-fine chest without being too conspicuous that I was mapping his body.

"I have a thing for Superman. Clark Kent is her daytime costume."

That made me smile. I pressed a dry kiss to the corner of his mouth.

"Why'd you even ask me out?" Before he could get the wrong idea, I quickly added, "I'm glad, but I didn't think you knew I existed before the Quinn thing."

Shawn paused to collect his thoughts, his brow furrowing into a trillion lines. He shifted beneath me like I'd made him uncomfortable.

My big fat stupid mouth.

I started to get up off him, but he shook his head and guided my face back to his chest, which was great, because I liked his chest. It was a really nice place to hang out, and my head settled into the crook of his shoulder nicely. "It wasn't supposed to be a date when we grabbed food but it turned into one at some point? I mean, I'd just—with Quinn, you know? I thought we should talk about what happened, I wanted to thank you for helping me out, and when I realized how cool you were, I wanted to spend more time with you. I always knew you were cool. Your T-shirts were fun. I guess I just saw an opening and went for it. I hope you don't think badly of me because of it. Because of what happened with Quinn."

I perched my chin on his chest so I could look right at him. "I don't. That was then, this is now, and now I'm happy. It's been great hanging out with you."

There was a heartbeat of a pause before Shawn dropped his head to whisper in my ear, "Happy is how you deserve to feel, Emma. I'm happy, too."

I floated into my house at quarter of ten, the night a whirlwind of laughing, dancing and kissing. It didn't even matter that half of my junior class thought I was a butt freak. I'd gone out with Shawn a second time, it was awesome and he asked me to the movies the following Friday. The niggling worry that this was a cosmic joke at my expense, that I'd have a Carrie-esque vat of pig's blood dropped on my head any day now, faded kiss by kiss.

"How was your night?" Mom asked from her usual perch on the couch.

Karen was at her side, tucked beneath a shared blanket. It seemed they'd had an Adult Conversation while I was gone and had come to an accord. Maybe Quinn-based Momageddon had been avoided after all.

"Good. Great. Thanks."

I flashed them a ten-billion-watt smile and headed for the fridge to forage for food. The mac and cheese had been fine, but that was hours ago and I needed to refuel. "Heading up to bed. Got another date next week, though."

"Do we get to meet him at some point?" Mom asked.

"Sure. When I'm convinced neither of you will terrify him." I popped back into the living room to offer cheek kisses before scrambling upstairs with my grape tomatoes and ranch dressing. The moment my foot hit the landing,

Versace appeared—not from Quinn's open doorway, but mine. He tensed, he hopped, he spun in a circle, he sat on the floor. It was all very confusing and very Small Doggish of him.

"What is it, boy? Is Timmy stuck in the well?"

Canine head tilt.

Oh. Right. Feeding time.

I turned tail to get his meal, plating it and dropping it in Quinn's room. He darted past me, making a disgusting snarfy noise with every bite. I'd have to clean up his puppy pee pad, but I allowed myself to enjoy my snack first, plunking down at my desk to do just that, bracing for another rousing round of Delete the Porno from the iPhone.

I was lucky. There had been only one inappropriate picture since dinner!

A check of Snapchat showed Laney and Tommy kissing in a cemetery because apparently that was a thing they did on Sundays for fun. Nikki's Twitter was full of vague messages about how much she liked her new girlfriend with the Big G. Facebook was my extended family members posturing about politics and linking animal pictures and recipes. The world, despite my tarnished reputation and amazing date with Shawn, had kept on turning. There was comfort in the normalcy. Everything had been so topsy-turvy with Quinn's departure, knowing a few rocks remained rocks was good for my headspace.

I plunked a tomato in my mouth as Versace reappeared in my room. He looked at me, looked at the tomato, groaned and then jumped up onto my hope chest so he could then jump onto my bed. There was a familiarity to the way he nestled into the blankets that suggested he'd determined my bed was his bed while I was out on my date.

"You're going to have to move, you realize."

The dog was unimpressed. He unhinged his jaw and yawned.

I finished stuffing my face, organized my books for the next day's classes and brushed my teeth. Then it was puppy pad maintenance, pajamas and a last check of my phone only to find a good-night with a smiley face text from Shawn. I returned in kind and approached the bed, nervous that a seven-pound dog would devour me. Surprisingly, Versace moved over to make space for my body. More surprisingly, after I turned out the light, he rested against the backs of my knees.

I peered down the bed. Moonlight let me see the beady, staring eyes of the food-swollen ankle hunter. He looked like a hairless gremlin, or maybe a tiny, enraged old man.

"Is that how it is? You can be bought with food?"

He dropped his chin onto his paws and closed his eyes.

CHAPTER NINETEEN

"THERE ARE WORSE THINGS TO BE THAN A BUTT SLUT," Nikki announced over her hamburger. The group was gathered around the lunch table at school, our trays neatly abutting our neighbor's so everyone had enough room. "Like, who cares if you are? It's your butt. You can do with it what you want."

"Slut shaming." Laney eyeballed her sandwich. Her black lipstick had transferred to the white bread and made it look like fungus grew around the bite mark. "That's what it is. Which is funny considering Quinn. Glass houses and all. It's no one's business who's banging who."

Tommy didn't have anything profound to add, so he offered me a French fry. I accepted it because French fries are delicious.

"I'm fine," I insisted. "The texts died down last night and I've only gotten a few comments today. People are staring, but that never killed anyone."

I focused on my grilled cheese, doing my damnedest to

convince myself that what I said wasn't utter crap. The pointing, snickering and whispering behind hands had been going on since the bus that morning. It wasn't pleasant, but as the day wore on it became less and less upsetting. I was nearly in tears by the end of first block. A whole block later, I only sort of wanted to flee the school.

"Oh, hey. Lookie here," Nikki said. She elbowed me in the side. I lifted my head, and approaching our table was not only Shawn, but J.T. and their friend Evan, too. Evan wore his football jersey to school almost every day, and today was no exception, except somehow during his food-wrangling he'd gotten ketchup all over the number on the front.

"These seats taken?" Shawn asked.

"All yours," I said. Shawn slid in beside me and pressed a kiss to my temple. J.T. and Evan took the free seats at that end of the table. It was a weird mix of jocks and nerds, but if the jocks didn't care, why would the nerds? We were a peaceful people. All outsiders were greeted with pocket protectors and Star Trek T-shirts.

Okay, no they weren't, but people probably thought that's what we did.

"Hey," Tommy said to Evan. He offered a wad of napkins, gesturing at his shirt. "You got something on...yeah."

Evan snatched them and dashed at the stain, frowning all the while. He was a mountain of a kid, as wide as a refrigerator, with a shock of ginger hair, freckles and skin so pale, he matched my milk. "Goddamn it. I don't have a backup."

"Don't worry! You're sitting with me and nobody's going to notice a stain in the presence of butt-tastic royalty." Everyone at the table paused to look at me. I was afraid my joke had gone flat, like humor as a coping mechanism was no longer de rigueur, but then Nikki snickered, Shawn grinned wolfishly and Tommy tittered into his napkin.

The only one not smiling was J.T. "Speaking of, I was off when you came by the house yesterday. I didn't mean—I was hungover. I was an asshole. Sorry about that."

"We're fine." I smiled at him and he smiled back, and like that, we were back to normal. Ish. There was nothing all that normal about Shawn's posse and mine sharing a lunch table. Except there was, too. There were plenty of common interests if you knew where to look for them. Movies, for one, and we talked about them for a good ten minutes, and then music for five more.

It was all going so swimmingly until Melody waltzed into the cafeteria with Josh at her side. I was pretty sure they weren't a couple, and yet he had his arm around her waist like they were, and I wondered what Quinn would say if she saw them like that—her best friend snuggled up to the guy whose dad she banged? Either she'd be furious one of her broom-riding sisters had scooped up her once-upon-a-time backup rich boy, or she'd be highly amused that Melody wanted her castoffs. It was a fifty-fifty.

Entwined, they passed our table, Melody's face going stony, Josh's smile tilting up on one side in a sneer.

"Sup, Hershey," he called, lifting his chin at me in a mock salute.

"Say it again." Shawn stood from his chair to face Josh, and in succession, J.T. and Evan stood with him, the three of them staring Josh down. It wasn't an ignorable display. In fact, the cafeteria quieted at the wall of Boy standing between me and Josh.

What the hell is happening?

"Like peacocks," Laney whispered behind me, and they were a bit like peacocks, fanning out their plumage for everyone to see.

And everyone saw.

"I was kidding," Josh said. His smiled wilted, his eyes large with distress. "It was a joke."

"It's not funny," Shawn said. "You feel me?"

Josh looked from Shawn to the other boys and then down at me. He blinked and cleared his throat. The smile plastered across his face was as tepid as old dishwater. "I feel you. We're cool."

"Then we're cool. Enjoy your lunch, man."

Shawn sat down. J.T. and Evan sat down. Josh and Melody scurried away.

I probably should have resented any implication that I couldn't handle the Josh situation myself, but I wasn't going to look a gift horse in the mouth. One public takedown by a couple of football players and the school took note. I wasn't so stupid as to think that's not exactly why Shawn brought his friends over to our table in the first place; Evan and J.T. ate with us only once a week after that despite Shawn sitting with me every day, but Shawn had his reasons for inviting them that day, and those reasons made my life more tolerable. I had only a handful more Hershey incidents as opposed to twenty an hour.

"Bullies only know one way to do things," Shawn said to me after Josh was out of earshot. "Sorry it came to that."

I forgave him. Of course I forgave him, and it proved to be one of the smarter things I'd ever done. Shawn and I became a couple over the next few weeks—not just people who dated or hung out on the weekends, but he called me his girlfriend, I got to call him my boyfriend and things were going great. I introduced him to my parents over Christmas break because my mother would not shut up about it, and despite knowing about the Quinn situation, she took to him immediately. He was polite and friendly and smart. He had a vision for the future. He treated me like gold.

All things Mom—and Karen—respected.

"I can only hope Quinn finds someone so cool," Karen said after he left. Then she sighed. She was having a hard time without Quinn around. Quinn barely took her phone calls, and when she did, it was usually Quinn lambasting Karen for some imaginary slight or another. I felt sorry for her. Not enough to want Quinn back in the house, but enough that I treated Karen with some extra TLC because she was a good person in a bad situation.

My dad popped in as a surprise on Christmas Eve, when Shawn was at the house. It wasn't much of a meeting—Dad had to fly back to Dubai the next morning, but for a few hours we sat, and talked, and joked like it hadn't been months since I'd seen him last. When he took off that night, leaving me feeling like it wasn't enough time, Shawn hugged me while I cried. I missed my dad. He'd promised he'd be more available soon, but he'd said that a lot since the divorce. I wanted to believe him. I just didn't.

Quinn wasn't the only one in the family with dad issues. The difference between me and her was I didn't punish the rest of the world with mine.

I didn't get to meet Shawn's parents until the beginning of February. I was worried he'd delayed because he didn't take me seriously or he thought they'd hate me, but Shawn explained it had to do with his little brother Max. His mom was an elementary school teacher in the town beside ours, his dad was an electrician and Max was a sweet little boy… when he was on his medication. Max had some emotional challenges and could be loud and violent on a bad day. His parents didn't want to introduce me to the mix until they could be sure that Max could handle me and that I could handle Max.

It wasn't an awful meeting. Max showed me his trillion Matchbox cars, I pretended to care as he rattled off their various characteristics and we ate spaghetti dinner afterward. Mr. and Mrs. Willis were really nice.

Come March, even the dog had turned around. He was my fuzzy little snuggle monkey. I could pick him up and carry him without dire consequence to my face parts. I walked him after school every day, let him sleep with me at night and even dressed him in the ridiculous sweaters Quinn bought him when he got cold.

Everything was going *so amazingly well.*

Which was why, when the front door of the house opened one Saturday morning and Quinn came marching in with an armload of luggage, I wanted to collapse to the floor and scream.

CHAPTER TWENTY

"HELLO, FAMILY!" ECHOED THROUGH THE HOUSE. QUINN'S arms were raised to the ceiling, her body turned in a ta-da! pose that would have been adorable on anyone else.

Karen wasn't home. It was me and my mom, and both of us looked at the blonde in our midst like she'd come to deliver us herpes by hand.

"Quinn? What are you—" Mom didn't finish the question. Alan strolled up our front walkway, face more orange than the last time I'd seen him, suggesting he was that many inches closer to actually becoming an Oompa Loompa. One of his hands worried at the collar of his shirt. The other toyed with the keys to his fancy new convertible.

"Dana. Emma. Hello," he said. "Where's Karen? We have a situation."

"Apparently so. She's at work, but I'd sit tight because I'm calling her. I'm not sure this is going to work," my mother said bluntly. "Quinn left on terrible terms."

Quinn's good cheer dissolved. She looked ready to cry

when she swung her head between my mother and her father. "What does that mean?"

"Let us work it out, Quinn. Sit down."

She did as he said, at the kitchen table, no argument.

Mom and Alan disappeared into the office.

That left me alone with the banshee. I looked at her. She looked at me, her eyes swollen and glassy like she'd done a whole heck of a lot of crying recently. I promptly stomped up to my bedroom and shut the door. I had no idea what to say to her.

This is a freak circumstance. A fight, a temporary setback.

But that's a whole lot of suitcases.

Versace whined at me from the bed. I picked him up, put him in my lap and proceeded to murder *the crap* out of video-game Nazis for the next few hours. At no point did anyone disturb me. My dog slept soundly. I could, through absolute sensory overload, pretend my Quinn-free utopia would see another day.

Until Karen and Mom showed their faces at suppertime. I had on my noise-canceling headphones, so I hadn't heard Karen come home, nor the family talking with Alan, nor anything from Quinn. Only Versace's growly, failed attempt at protecting me from potential enemies clued me in that I had to pay attention to the real world. I paused the game and barked, "Come in."

It must have been flinty because the dog hopped off my lap to curl up in my laundry, eyes bulging from his skull.

"Hey. Can we come in?" Mom asked from the doorway.

"That depends on what you're about to tell me."

Karen cringed over Mom's shoulder.

Oh, here we go.

I motioned them inside, but didn't say anything. They parked themselves, hip touching hip, on my bed. Karen wrung her hands. My mother had the best and worst poker face in the world; it was good because it belied nothing. It was bad because she only used it when bad things were afoot.

Like Quinn.

"There was a fight. A fistfight. Between Quinn and her stepmother."

"What'd Quinn do?"

Not what did the stepmother do, but what did Quinn do, because I knew who'd started the shitshow. I think the moms did, too, as they both looked distinctly uncomfortable.

"I won't go into details, but it takes two to fight. Hannah rose to the occasion and hit Quinn. Alan's uncomfortable having them in the house together and I can't say I totally disagree." Karen sighed. "It will be conditional, Emma. If she acts out or… There will be conditions."

"And she'll honor those conditions for how long?" I demanded.

Karen grimaced.

"You can't enforce conditions, Karen," I continued. "I'm not trying to be a jerk, but let's be real. You couldn't even keep her on the phone when she was at Alan's. Did she ever get therapy like you asked?"

"No," Karen admitted quietly. "But that's one of the conditions."

"Uh-huh." I peered down at the dog who was mine for a short time but probably wouldn't be within a few hours. It made me sad to think about. "So let's skip ahead. You come in here and tell me she's coming back conditionally, and I'll tell you that conditional won't last, and then you'll promise me it'll change. And the change won't happen, and I'll point that out in a couple weeks when it's back to how it was, and then the argument will be you can't let your daughter be homeless, and I'll concede the point, and Quinn gets to stay no matter how good or bad she is. This isn't a dialogue. This is you telling me she's coming back. I guess my choice is whether or not I want to stay. I'm going to call Dad and see when he's done with his Dubai contract, because I'm pretty sure the answer is 'hell, no.'"

"Emma!" My mother and Karen both looked horrified.

"You're not going anywhere," Mom said. "This was your house first."

"You're right, it was, but you don't get to bring back someone who abused me and then tell me I have to live with it. Sorry, I've ridden that ride. Have the T-shirt. It sucked."

Karen babbled apologies that on a better day would have made me sympathetic toward her distress. It only served to annoy me more.

"We'll figure it out, I promise. I… I…" Karen choked her way through a sob, her fingers pinching the bridge of her nose. Mom took that opportunity to guide her out of the room, her face whipping between her near-wife and her daughter. She looked torn, like she wasn't sure which one of us needed her more at that very moment.

"Go with her," I said.

"Okay. Don't call your father yet. Please. We'll talk more with Alan and see what we can work out. I'm sorry, honey. So sorry." Mom looked like she might cry, too, which lent me some pause. Mom wasn't prone to tears, not like Karen, but apparently the notion of me taking off instead of staying in the house with Quinn scared her.

"Fine."

"Thank you."

All that was left was me, my angst and my snoring Chihuahua. I fired up my computer and messaged Nikki, who, to her credit, responded with a resounding OH COME ON when I told her Quinn had crawled out of the crypt to plague us once again.

Did her dad get sick of her or something? WTF.

Better. Fistfight with her stepmom, I replied.

Wow. What a douche bag.

Yep. Queen Vinegar of Douche Mountain.

We back and forthed awhile longer, but then Nikki had to go to Justice's practice because they were, after three and a half months, still seeing one another and sitting through boring sports things was a high school relationship obligation. I knew this because I dated a football player. A ballerina-slash-football player, but still. I'd gone to every game over the winter, cheering for the blue jerseys even though I had no idea why nearly grown men were flopping around on top of one another. I was also still clueless what a down was.

The spring had brought baseball into Shawn's life, which meant he wouldn't be available to me until suppertime. Laney and Tommy were both working until three, so I couldn't bother them, either. Tommy had picked up a part-time job at the Bear after February break, making him the token dude employee on an all-girl staff. He didn't seem to mind it too much even if his lavender-colored hat looked silly as hell.

"I think it's cute," Laney told him. "That's all that matters."

She had a point.

Alone and wallowing in Quinn despair, I turned to homework for distraction. I had a five-page Napoleon paper due at the end of next week, and Waterloo wasn't writing itself no matter how much I wished it would.

I'd gotten about two pages down when my mother resurfaced, this time alone, her knock on my door tentative.

"Come in," I managed.

She slunk in like a thief—head down, shoulders tense, her hands buried in her pockets—as she plunked down onto my bed. She sucked in a deep breath, waiting patiently for me to turn around, but I kept right on scribbling, mustering zero enthusiasm for the conversation.

"We might have a solution," Mom said.

"I'm listening."

"She'll finish her junior year here because the situation at Alan's needs to simmer down. Alan has agreed to take her back in June and July. If Quinn can behave herself, she'll be allowed to come home in August so she can start cheerleading with the rest of the squad. If she can't, Karen's looking into boarding schools for girls with behavioral problems. Quinn seems suitably cowed by the idea.

"Therapy, too," Mom added. "She's agreed to go with both of her parents. It's been made perfectly clear she needs to leave you alone. I told her I wouldn't put up with it, and I'm much harder to please than Karen is."

"Uh-huh."

I never lifted my head so Mom was, effectively, talking to my back. Normally that'd get me in trouble, but she was cutting me some slack considering the circumstances.

"Does that sound fair? We're trying to find something that'll work for everyone. It's hard. Impossible, really."

I scowled, the words on the page before me blurring into squiggly nonsense lines.

I hate you, Napoleon.

"Whatever you think is best. I'll give it a shot, but I'm not putting up with any more abuse. It was too nice around here when she was gone."

"It was," Mom admitted. She stood so she could hug me from behind, her lips pressed to the top of my head. There was a desperation to her grip, her arms too clingy, and I dropped my pencil to put my hands over her forearms. I loved my mom. I liked living with her when Quinn wasn't a constant worry. I didn't want to leave her to go to Dad's, but I would if it meant living without demon spawn.

"I love you," she said quietly.

"I know."

CHAPTER TWENTY-ONE

QUINN MADE HER FIRST STAB AT CONTACT BEFORE supper. I could hear thuds echoing down the hall followed by snippets of quiet conversation between her and Karen. Quinn's voice broke down walls on a normal day, reaching decibels far too great for one mortal mouth, but for once, she was muted.

Maybe the threat of The School for Wayward Drama Queens had sunk in.

I was finishing up my history paper when the double knock came.

"Yep."

Quinn poked her head inside. She looked better, less soggy than earlier, her hair in a ponytail, her face washed clean of makeup. Fresh pajamas and socks softened her usual diva-ness.

"Hey. I was hoping to see Versace."

The dog jumped at her voice and darted over to her. She

cooed, she squealed, she covered him in sweet kisses. He loved it, writhing in delight in her arms.

"Who's my sweet baby? Who?"

She wandered out with him in her arms.

"You might want to take his stuff," I called after her.

"Oh, right."

At no point did she thank me for taking care of her dog while she was gone. Karen and Mom had talked about giving him over to a rescue organization, but once he'd warmed up to me, I told them I'd take ownership. He'd become my dog in that pie-slice of time when Quinn didn't factor into my life. Did Quinn notice? No, of course not, but she did sweep right in and pick up like those months of care were meaningless.

She'd just grabbed his dog bed when I offered a pointed, "You're welcome."

"Huh?" She stopped and blinked at me, the dog cradled against her boobs. He wiggled, looking between her and me and back again.

"They were going to get rid of him. He doesn't like either of our moms. I convinced them to keep him and made sure he got fed. You're welcome."

"Oh. Thanks."

She smiled at me, too saccharine to be earnest, and disappeared with the dog, whispering into Versace's radial ears all the while.

I tapped my pencil against my notebook, willing myself not to charge after her and scream at her for being so ungrateful. So presumptuous. So *Quinn*. Everything about her annoyed me. But then a funny thing happened to improve my festering mood.

Versace came back.

She'd moved all his stuff into her room, had taken him in with her, and he'd promptly trotted my way to settle into a pair of abandoned jeans on my floor. I could hear her making kissy noises, his name singsong from her lips, but no dog answered the summons. He curled up and closed his eyes. I smiled at his wonderful, ugly body. Then I got up, walked down the hall and entered Quinn's domain without hesitation.

I never would have done it months ago *but I wasn't afraid of her anymore*. Something was different since the last time she'd lived there. Shawn? Maybe. But I was pretty sure it was more than that, too. It was me. I was more confident. More willing to speak up and put my foot down when I was unhappy.

Maybe the smear campaign had thickened my skin.

"I'm going to grab his pee pad. He might need some time to adjust," I said, my voice flat.

Quinn looked bewildered. Then she looked mad. "Whatever. He'll be back or he won't. I don't care. I've got too much to do to worry about a rodent."

She waved her hand at her room. Suitcases were strewed across the floor like they'd been flung there by a tornado. Clothes were half on hangers, half off. Her dresser drawers were open, bags covering the bureau top, desk and vanity. Lacy underwear peppered the bed like pastel-colored confetti.

"I've got a lot of unpacking to do. Daddy bought me a whole new wardrobe and I haven't had time to sort out the old stuff I don't want anymore." She eyeballed me as I rolled up the puppy pad. "It's too bad you aren't my size. I'd have a lot of stuff for you."

"Yeah, too bad," I spit.

She's being civil. If you have to live with her, you can be civil back.

I cleared my throat. "Thanks anyway. I'm sure Melody would be interested."

"Oh, probably. She's always drooled over my clothes. I gave her a Fendi one time and I thought she'd wet her pants."

"What's a Fendi?"

"A purse. A designer. It was a five-hundred-dollar bag but I liked my Prada way better. Like, same color and everything and the Prada was almost fifteen hundred, you know?"

No, I don't know. I thought it was a car.

"Cool." I headed for the door, ready to escape to the safety of my room, where the only thing worth fifteen hundred bucks was maybe my computer and tablet combined, when Quinn asked, "How's Shawn? Melody said you two are still going strong."

Every muscle in my body furled. Without Quinn, I may not have gotten to know Shawn, but she'd also used him, exploited him and, when I'd warned him about it, gone out of her way to ruin my reputation. This was not, nor would it ever be, a happy conversation piece between us.

"It's… We are. It's good." I turned to stare at her, the pee pad clutched in my hand. "We've been dating a few months now."

She nodded, her fingers running over the top of the nearest suitcase. "I screwed that up. Like, he's a good guy. Hot, too. I didn't know he liked thick girls, but hey. Black guy.

Big surprise, right? At least you finally popped your cherry. Good on you."

I winced, partially for the stereotype, partially because she was getting too close to something she had no business being near.

"Well, he likes me and I like him. I'm not sure being thick has anything to do with it. But…uh." I scrambled for something to say that wasn't *Whyfor did you return from hell, foul beast* and settled on, "I gotta take care of the dog. Leave your door open, though. In case he wants to come back."

"He won't," Quinn said to my retreating back. "No one ever does."

Quinn's return translated to massive anxiety for me. I had two concerns I couldn't shake. The first was that things would settle into the same old pattern of her screeching for satisfaction and us relenting because she held us hostage. The second was that she'd try to make nice with me. I'd allowed her to win me over once before only to be burned when she outed Nikki. Round two was not happening.

Fortunately, the impending graduation of the cheerleading captain spared me. Quinn was *obsessed* with locking up the captainship of the squad for the next year, like the only thing that mattered in her world besides reestablishing herself at the top of the Westvale food chain was the mantle of Cheerleading Queen. Her three-month departure meant she'd lost some of her established power, though, which left Justice the heir apparent.

Quinn had other ideas.

"I'm better than her. Plus, she's getting fat. No one wants

to catch a fatty in a basket toss," Quinn announced at the dinner table.

Keeping my mouth shut. Keeping my mouth shut. Keeping my mouth shut.

"That's such an awful word. Do you have to use it?" Karen chastised, passing the macaroni salad. Quinn reared away like carbohydrates could bite. It was so over-the-top, I snickered. Two seconds later, Mom's sneaker made contact with my ankle. I bit my tongue so I didn't giggle aloud.

"I call it like I see it, Mom. Her thighs look like cottage cheese. If you take the sport seriously, have the consideration to watch your weight. Other people have to lift you. Like, I know it's hard to turn down food sometimes. Ask Emma. She's got an eating disorder."

I'd been merrily slopping macaroni salad onto my plate before she said that, but the jab stopped me short. I had an eating disorder? Since when? I peered at Quinn, spoon poised. She motioned at me enthusiastically.

"No one's Emma's size by choice. She can't help it. But you know what's awesome about Emma? She's not pretending to be a cheerleader. She sticks to nonathletic stuff. Like reading. She can eat fifty pounds of macaroni salad and it doesn't matter."

"For God's sake, Quinn. Don't be so rude," Karen snapped. "You've been gone for months. Can't you try to be nice?"

"I was being nice!" Quinn insisted. "That was a compliment! And if Emma ever wants to take off some tonnage, I will totally help her."

Yes, I felt super complimented as I put back half of my macaroni salad and slid the bowl to my mother. Both moms frowned at Quinn, but she only rolled her eyes, her fork stabbing a piece of broccoli.

"None of you get it," she proclaimed.

She was right—I didn't, nor did I want to. I liked Justice a whole heck of a lot more than I liked Quinn. So I held my tongue and tucked into my macaroni salad, trying hard not to think about my own ever-expanding cottage-cheese thighs.

Over the next few weeks, I prepared for my SATs, worked on my science fair project in the garage and caught up on my reading for AP English. Quinn blatantly ignored every school obligation she had to concentrate on cheerleading. By the time spring competition season started in May, she proclaimed herself in top shape.

"I'm down twelve pounds since the end of school last year. It's these low-carb shakes I've been getting. They work way better than ex-lax purging, which gets disgusting." Quinn stopped filing her nails at the bus stop to eyeball me, leaning back to look at my butt. I looked at it, too, in case I'd sat in something, but no. It was another indication that she found my cellulite repugnant. "If you're interested."

I refused to answer, instead looking down the street longingly, hoping to see the bus, but it failed me. Quinn took that as her cue to continue blabbing.

"I like the coffee ones, but Melody gets the chocolate ones, and I know you like chocolate. Anyway, if you want some, I'll pick up an extra case. You drink one for breakfast and one for lunch. I'm pushing them to the squad today. Maybe if Justice goes on a crash diet, it won't be like trying to lift an elephant during pyramids."

Still I said nothing, but she didn't care. Half of the time Quinn talked to me, she talked *at* me. I didn't need to be a willing participant in the conversation. I needed to be in the vicinity and have ears. Pulse was totally optional.

Despite my lack of interest, Quinn lugged a mountain of low-carb shakes into my room that night. I sat at my desk finalizing my science project plan while she heaved, hauled and grunted two heavy-looking cases into the corner.

"Don't get up and help or anything. Jesus," she complained. "I only did you a favor."

I looked from the shakes to their purchaser before going back to my design. I had a piece of tape stuck to my forearm and I brushed it aside, but it clung anyway. "You've been on such a weight-loss kick, I figured the exercise was good for you. Might take off another half a pound," I said.

"Hardy *harr.*" She yanked the tape off my forearm, taking my arm hair with it. I cringed and glowered at her, rubbing the sore spot, but she just traipsed back into the hall. "I'm trying to help you. Your IBM is probably a billion."

It took me a second to figure out that IBM was BMI.

Sometimes she was so dumb, she made me fear for the future of our species.

"It's body mass index, not… You know what, never mind," I said, flipping over my paper to work on the second half. "You're obsessed with my weight. I'm not obsessed, Shawn's not obsessed, but you are. Why?"

"I'm a helper. Speaking of which, you'll want to chill the shakes before you drink them. They taste chalky, but no pain, no gain. It works so good, but don't eat forty cheeseburgers a week."

Before I could retort, she was bounding off to her room. I eyeballed the diet shakes. So did the dog. He sniffed them and growled before jumping onto my bed to stare at them hatefully.

"Good dog," I said.

He wagged.

I went back to sketching plants in jars, but then I caught a reflection of the shakes in the mirror on the back of my door. For a moment, I wondered what life would be like at size eight. Maybe I'd look hotter. Maybe I could eat without wondering if people were mentally criticizing my food choices. Swimwear wouldn't be the bane of my existence. I could get one of those cute navel piercings without my flab rolls eating the dangling belly charm.

All of that contributed to my sip of that first shake.

The taste of salt, dirt and despair contributed to my spitting out said first sip.

All over my project design, too, which meant I'd be redrawing it as soon as I recovered from the shock of putting something so vile in my mouth. No wonder Quinn lost twelve pounds. That magical elixir of weight loss probably dissolved the inside of her mouth until nothing would taste good ever again. I escaped to the bathroom, surreptitiously pouring Ye Olde Nasty down the drain all the while hoping Quinn wouldn't emerge from her room to ask questions.

I swore then and there that this was my first and last low-carb experiment. Sadly, my solemn vow wasn't enough to put an end to the ordeal.

Every day, Quinn checked in with me—breakfast, lunch, art class. "Did you drink one yet?" I wouldn't outright tell her that I refused to imbibe Satan's pee water because arguing with her was a waste of time, but it was getting stupid.

Stupider. Low-carb living was the only thing on her mind whenever we crossed paths.

"Don't get discouraged. You'll see results soon. You have so much to lose is all," she said, patting me on the shoulder. I batted her away and stalked off, but she didn't take the hint. For three weeks, she didn't take the hint. I figured sooner or later she'd look at the remaining shakes in my room and realize they were all accounted for, but no. She wasn't that perceptive.

It was the spring pep rally that saved me. Quinn's cheerleading coup hadn't gone as planned. Justice was still running the show, giant thighs and all, and the official vote for the captain of the squad was supposed to happen after the regional cheer competition. I didn't know this until Quinn came marching into my room to half tell, half shriek it at me. Her cheeks were pink, her head tilted in a way that suggested the hamsters inside her skull were furiously pounding away at their wheels.

"This situation is so dumb. I am *so* much better. Melody says so. Jill says so. Everyone says so, but they're too chickenshit to oust the fatty." There was a momentary pause before she added, "No offense or anything."

"Uh-huh," I said from behind my desk. "Justice is a nice girl."

Quinn threw herself across my bed, arms sprawled to either side. She peered at my ceiling, sullen and contemplative. "This is a sport and sports aren't fun if you don't win. There's no room for nice here. The squad will be miserable if she sticks around."

I snorted. "I've never heard of niceness being a problem

before. In any venue, even sports. And if something isn't fun, I'm not sure why you'd invest so much energy into it."

Her nostrils flared as she propped herself up on her elbow, peering down her body to stare at the untouched cases of chocolate shake in the corner. A long silence stretched between us. I braced, expecting her to freak out at me for how many were left, but she oozed off my mattress to grab the top flat, *oomph*ing as she hoisted them.

"I need these, if you don't mind? I'll leave the other pack," she said. I nodded voraciously, vaguely recalling her mentioning something about preferring the coffee shakes, but who was I to ask questions? She was taking away the canned evil without argument.

"Sure."

She eased toward my door, pausing on the threshold to cast me a smile over her shoulder. It wasn't a nice smile. Her eyes were narrowed, her teeth all white and shiny like a piranha. Her tongue came out to glide over her bottom lip, her shoulders lifting as she burst into giggles.

"I just had the best idea," she said.

"Huh?"

She didn't explain, instead tottering toward her villain lair, her laughter echoing through the upstairs hall. She was up to something, and already I didn't like it. I refused to throw Justice to the wolves, not even in the name of a domestic peace treaty, so I followed Quinn to her room and leaned in her doorway.

"Don't," I warned. "Whatever it is you're thinking of doing. Don't."

"What?" Quinn was too busy opening the chocolate shakes to pay me any mind.

"Justice is my friend."

"Since when?"

Since she started boffing Nikki.

But I couldn't say that so I settled for, "She's been hanging out since you've been gone. I don't want drama."

"You worry too much."

"I mean it, Quinn," I warned. "Leave her alone or we're going to have a problem. I'll bring it to our moms and you know what that means."

That got her attention. Her head whipped around, hard and fast like the girl from *The Exorcist*. She glowered at me, her color rising, but I wouldn't look away. Not when her lip curled. Not when she sputtered angrily. I saw the nastiness bubbling just below the surface, threatening to fork her tongue, and I braced for a torrent of awfulness, except…

"Whatever, Emilia. Don't worry about it." She flopped on the floor and busied herself with her latest pair of shoes, refusing to look at me.

"You're sure?"

"Yes, I'm sure! Now go away."

CHAPTER TWENTY-TWO

I'M THE ANTI-ATHLETE. IT'S NOT THAT I DON'T LIKE sports, I'm simply terrible at them.

Mom put me in softball at eight. I was the kid who took the ball to the face and lost a tooth. I was also the kid who got so excited after I hit the ball that I threw the bat and cranked the umpire, Mr. Reynolds, in the privates. Mom stopped insisting I try out sports after that, mostly because she saw Mr. Reynolds at the grocery store from time to time and still got embarrassed thinking about him rolling on the ground holding his injured sack.

This was never *a thing* for me. I didn't feel unfulfilled without team sports. I occupied my time with other school activities and had no exclusion hang-ups about my lack of athleticism. However, I was painfully ignorant of how sports worked. Which sport was played when. What divisions meant. How competitions were handled. Dating Shawn helped with that some—basketball and baseball were pretty easy to understand even if football was horribly confusing—but cheerleading was a whole other kettle of fish. When Quinn's cheer squad won divisions, I needed an explanation of why this was such a big deal.

Unfortunately, Quinn was the one who explained it to me.

"Westvale is a tiny shithole school. Our team gets put in with other tiny shithole schools in Division Five East. Last weekend, all the tiny shitholes got together to compete and we won the East title. So now we go to a competition with the other Division Five winners across the state," she said. "And the best of those go to state finals to compete with real schools."

"Competing for what? Best shithole?" I asked. We were in the backseat of the car, on our way to a steak house for dinner with our moms. Quinn had her head dipped forward so she could text her friends. Her hair spilled down in a shimmery veil, hiding her face, which was probably good because I was sure she wasn't pleased with my question. I didn't need death-by-laser-eyes.

"Hi! Parents in the front seat. Can we stop the pointless swearing?" my mom demanded.

"Soz," Quinn said.

"Yeah. Soz," I repeated. My mother's eyes swept my way in the rearview mirror. It wasn't a friendly look. I grinned anyway.

Asking Quinn about cheerleading got her talking. And talking. And talking. She spent all of dinner explaining how competitions worked. I nodded like I found it all so very interesting, but that was only because I'd put myself on my mother's radar with my sarcasm. I had to be nice to Quinn so I wasn't murdered by Mommy.

Of course, being dead might have gotten me out of going to the competition, but Mom probably would have dragged my moldering carcass along anyway to make a point.

Two weeks later, the Division Five Finals became an unfortunate reality. We were *up and at 'em* at five o'clock in the morning so we'd make it to the hosting university before eight. The two-hour drive was given an hour of extra padding because Karen was a fascist. I attempted to fall asleep in the car, but Quinn was so excited all she did was talk. And talk. And talk. She spewed words with few breaks for air. It was one nonsensical observation about the team after another.

This one was too skinny.

That one didn't kick her leg high enough.

This one couldn't keep time but at least her acrobatics were good.

That one had a huge cold sore and did we know that was a form of herpes and *how gross is that?*

And, of course, "Justice is still too fat."

Which she wasn't, but I wasn't going to argue with Quinn at five in the morning on a Saturday.

My moms pretended to give a damn about what she was saying, asking questions here and there to keep Quinn engaged probably so she wouldn't whine about the long drive. It did nothing for my sleep agenda. I had to swallow a rather emphatic request for all of them to shut their traps because decent human beings weren't supposed to be functioning at this hour, much less conversing about cheerleading.

We pulled into the university parking lot at eight, cars stretching out as far as the eye could see. I followed my family to the closest brick building. I'd yet to meet a fat, socially stymied cheerleader; they were all lithe and pretty and popular. The prospect of being the lonely nerd girl amidst a murder of cheerleaders made me want to gargle with Drano.

"Chin up," Karen said, her elbow nudging at my ribs. "We're here for support. Later, we'll get sundaes."

That did make it a little more tolerable. So did the thought of getting to talk to Justice. I did like her.

Our moms had to take care of Quinn's registration, which left me helping Quinn with her various and sundry bags. I schlepped along behind her, a duffel bag in one hand, the remains of my drive-through coffee in the other. I had on sunglasses because the day star burned. Also because it was easier to hide from people that way. I didn't have to make eye contact like a human.

"Does this make me your caddy?" I asked Quinn's back, her ponytail high and bobbing with every step.

"Huh? No, you're not catty. You can be a bitch, but that's only sometimes," was the response.

I couldn't tell if she misheard me or if she really didn't know what a caddy was. If it was the latter, I was better off not knowing. I followed her down a long corridor, to a door adorned with a piece of pink poster board with sparkle paints and foil stars on it saying Welcome Westvale. I thought I'd hand over Quinn's stuff and then go find Mom and Karen, but Quinn walked inside and held the door open with her foot so it didn't slam me in the face. It was considerate of her. Sort of. She was probably protecting her luggage.

The room was nothing special—a classroom with the desks pushed up against the opposite wall, the chairs upended for better storage. Fold-out tables lined the front, beneath the chalkboard, covered with makeup, hair products, pom-poms and various uniform necessities. I saw ankle socks, pleated skirts, half shirts and those fancy underwear things the girls wore so their acrobatics weren't arrest-worthy.

There were also stacks and stacks of low-carbohydrate shakes. Oh, and cheerleaders. Lots and lots of those floating around in excited, tittering clusters. And every girl in the room appeared to be on the low-carb kick. Even Justice. She'd just opened a can when she waved me over.

"Hey! Maybe next competition you can convince Nikki to come. She said something about rather flushing her head in the toilet repeatedly."

"That's my girl." I motioned at the shake. "You're on that now, too?"

Justice snorted. "Not often. Sometimes, but I have to be careful. Quinn hands them out like candy. I figured I'd drink one to keep her quiet. It tastes like ass."

"Yeah, it does."

Behind us, Quinn blathered to her teammates. Trumpeting cheers followed. I made my excuses so I wouldn't have to listen to any more squealing. It was a cross between cats in heat and police sirens. I found my moms seated in a stuffy auditorium with too-hot lighting, the complimentary cups of lemonade doing little to offset the crammed-in bodies. I dozed off for the first hour. So did my mom, though she'd never admit it. Karen was the only one who managed to look interested in the ceremonial proceedings.

She can be stalwart, that one. A real Viking woman.

I woke up for the first team's routine an hour later when their music nearly blasted off the doors. Despite the morning's misgivings, I couldn't look away. The girls were real athletes who pulled off some physics-defying stunts that had me holding my breath in places. I even texted Shawn to tell him that I hadn't at any point wanted to gouge out my eyes, to which he responded, Good, I plan to look at them later.

Which was more proof that I had an awesome boyfriend.

I was midreply when Karen stood from her seat, her phone clasped in her hand. "I'll be back. Quinn wasn't feeling great before we left and she needs more medicine than what we brought."

"Is she okay?" my mom asked.

"She will be." Karen motioned to her stomach. "Stomach problem. I'll be back shortly. I saw a pharmacy up the road."

I didn't think anything of it, not when Karen left, not when Karen sat back down, not when the next team went through their routines.

No, I didn't think anything of it until the Westvale team ran out onto the gymnasium floor hours later. The girls were done up, all pretty and perky. Quinn was toward the back, smiling brightly, her lips scarlet red against her ivory skin. Justice was the shortest of them, her dark head barely cresting five feet, which put her at the center of the squad in the front row.

She didn't look good—she was pale and kept covering her mouth with her miniature pom-pom. At one point, she hunched over and shook her head before bouncing up again, the smile on her mouth so forced it looked like a grimace. As the squad counted down from three to break into their routine, their voices ringing out, she wobbled on her feet, her kicks not as energetic as those of her compatriots.

I watched the performance with both fascination and

dread. The first because they really were good at what they did and the extra weeks of practice had paid off, the second because Justice withered while Quinn thrived. At one point, Justice had to stop middance, and one of the girls leaned over to check on her, but Justice shook her off, jumping back into the routine despite her discomfort.

"That girl doesn't look good," my mother remarked. "Is she sick?"

"I don't know. She was fine earlier," I said seconds before *it* happened.

By *it* I mean Justice being tossed in the air and yelping as the girls caught her. She looked panicked, screamed for them to stop as they lifted her into the air for a second round. To their credit, the squad did stop midstunt, but once someone is thrown you have to catch them. And they did catch her only…

Well. Shitpocalypse. There is no other way to describe it. On Justice, on the two girls that caught her. A fecal fiesta.

It happened so fast it took a while for everyone to process the unleashed horror. There were gasps, some heaves, a few muffled groans, a giggle or two and then silence. Pure, perfect silence as the girls that caught the exploding cheerleader realized what happened, screamed and promptly wailed which—if I was being fair—I probably would have cried, too.

Justice started sobbing. Her mother ran onto the gym floor, pulling off her coat to wrap it around her soiled daughter. It would have been a terribly sad thing to witness if the circumstances weren't so very disorienting. Some cheerleaders drifted off to talk among themselves. Others fled to their parents. Like the cheese, Quinn stood alone. Her eyes scanned the bleachers, watching people's faces, absorbing their reactions.

She was the only one smiling.

CHAPTER TWENTY-THREE

"I'M GOING TO KILL HER," I RASPED.

It was not the reaction Mom expected in the wake of Justice's trauma. Her head whipped my way, but all my attention was focused on Karen.

"What's going on?" Mom demanded.

I grabbed Karen's wrist. "Was the medicine ex-lax?"

"What?"

"The stomach medicine for Quinn. Was it ex-lax?"

"Yes. Why?"

I wanted to scream, *Because Justice was fine earlier. Because Justice is the one girl standing in the way of Quinn being cheerleading captain. Because Justice was drinking chocolate diet shakes Quinn handed out*, but I didn't have proof.

Come to find out, I didn't need it. Mom caught my drift and stiffened beside me. Karen looked between us before adding one and one and one and getting three.

They know.

I didn't speak. Neither mom asked me to. The competition was all but over—Westvale couldn't win in the wake of Shitpocalypse—so we headed out, Karen saddled with the unenviable task of collecting her spawn from the prep room. When Quinn climbed into the car with her duffel bag over her shoulder, she talked and talked and talked about the other routines, about the day, about anything other than what happened to Justice. She didn't breathe through fifteen straight minutes of diatribe. I was about to choke her, was actually envisioning my hands around her throat, until my mom snapped, "Enough, Quinn."

"Excuse me?"

Quinn sounded like she was ready to throw down with Mom, but then my mom whirled in the passenger side and pointed a finger in her face.

"Don't push me. Shut. Your. Mouth."

Karen kept driving. Quinn sputtered indignantly.

"Are you going to let her talk to me that way?"

"Yes," Karen said. "In fact, I am."

Quinn's mouth opened, then closed, then opened and closed again. She jerked her head my way. I could feel the weight as she peered at my profile but I was so angry I didn't trust myself not to whale on her if I met her gaze. I focused on the game on my phone, on the colors that blurred together but couldn't form pictures in the face of my rage. My hands shook. My heart pounded in my ears.

Twenty minutes away from the house, Karen sucked in a deep breath. "She could press charges, Quinn."

"Oh, we're talking now?" came Quinn's sharp reply.

"It's poisoning. Legal substance or not, it's poisoning." Karen sounded so tired when she added, "I won't defend you. So you'd best talk to your father if it comes to that."

Quinn's breath hitched. "I… Mom. What ar… I…" She cleared her throat, the color in her cheeks rising. "I don't know what you're talking about," she insisted. "I didn't do anything."

"Don't, Quinlan. I'm so exhausted."

Quinn had no retort. When we pulled into the driveway, she ran for the house to hide in her room, never making a peep. My moms cut me a wide berth. They knew I was friends with Justice. They knew that this, though not aimed at me, pushed the envelope too far. It wasn't an explicit break of their conditional Quinn acceptance, but it was close enough they couldn't sit idly by without addressing it. I guessed that's what they were doing when they went first to Quinn's room to talk to her and then to the office to talk among themselves.

Shawn said he'd save me by taking me out of the house that night, so I escaped to the garage to work on my science project. Three of my specimen plants were sequestered there, denied sunlight, so they could wither for scientific advancement. As I opened the side door, I heard a faint buzzing sound seconds before there was a sharp bite on the side of my neck.

"Shit!" I clapped my hand against the sting and bowed over from the waist. I'd been stung before, but it was a sensitive spot and I was already in a terrible mood. I collapsed to the ground, sitting in the grass, tears silently streaming down my face. The hateful hornet hovered nearby, and I watched it fly up into the gutter on the garage side. I wanted to blast it with Raid, but *a ladder* and *effort*. Pointless weeping suited me far better.

I didn't move from my spot until Shawn arrived.

"Hey. Babe. You okay?" He got out of the car and ran my way, crouching beside me. I lifted my face to him, a wilty, gross mess, but he gathered me in close and hugged me anyway. His lips grazed the top of my ear.

"I'm pretty sure Quinn drugged Justice," I croaked. It all poured out of me, the weeks leading up to the competition, the shakes, the ex-lax. Shawn sat with me on the ground, in the dimming daylight, his hands sliding and stroking and soothing over my back. The touch helped. Something in the world was right even if my neck hurt and my stepsister was out to ruin the world.

"Does Nikki know?" he asked.

"I'm sure Justice called her. I couldn't … I was so mad I couldn't talk. Or text. I shut down. Why's she like this?"

"Who knows? She's obviously got some issues," he said.

I allowed a dribble of humorless laughter. "She doesn't have issues, Shawn. She's got *volumes*."

I had plans with Nikki on Sunday but she canceled them to be with Justice. I couldn't complain considering the circumstances. Shawn had a family thing at his grandmother's across the state, and the Laney and Tommy faction were going to the movies to see a slasher flick. They invited me along, but I wasn't keen on playing third wheel, so I opted to stay home and work on my project.

I kept to the garage, wary of attack hornets and attack stepsisters.

The moms hadn't done anything about the Justice situation yet. It made for a tense, unwelcoming household. Quinn wasn't surfacing from her room. I wasn't particularly friendly nor would I be until I knew what the fallout was post-competition. I asked once, and my mother eyeballed me before saying, "We'll let you know when there's something to know. It's out of your hands." It was a quasi-pleasant way of telling me to mind my business.

It didn't sit well with me, not when I thought about all the promises made when Quinn had moved back in.

"Things will change," they'd said. "We won't tolerate her acting out."

Except by doing nothing, that's exactly what they were doing.

By the time Monday morning hit, I was in a full snit. Quinn was, yet again, going to get off scot-free. That she'd hurt people to get her way didn't matter, nor would it ever matter, because she was a sociopath.

She did little to relieve the notion.

The household ran on routine. My mothers got ready for work in the downstairs bathroom with my mom in the shower at six and Karen in the shower by six thirty. Upstairs, something similar was supposed to happen, except Quinn got up at five to go through her various beautification routines. More often than not, she cut into my half hour of bathroom time anyway.

I had to be in the shower by six so I could be downstairs by half past to eat breakfast and make the bus before seven. Quinn, however, was having a Quinn-scale crisis inside the bathroom and had locked it down like Alcatraz.

"It's, like, the biggest zit ever," I heard on the other side of the door.

"Cool. Pop it and let me in. It's five past," I said.

"You don't pop zits. That leaves a scar."

"This does not change the fact that you're making me late. Hurry up," I growled through clenched teeth.

"You'll live." I heard the clamor of cabinets opening then closing, one after the other. "God, where is my Murad?"

I glanced at the hall clock. It was closing in on ten past. If she didn't get out of there within the next two minutes, I was going to have to choose between being late, going hungry, or not showering, none of which pleased me. I wasn't a super generous soul first thing in the morning on a good day. Denying me my few luxuries on top of my existing aggravation ensured that I would devolve into a Bite-o-saurus Rex. "If you don't hurry up, I'm going to have to skip breakfast. Can't you de-zit in the comfort of your own room?"

There was another thud on the other side of the door as she rifled through the cabinets. "Have you looked at your ass lately, Emilia? I'm pretty sure skipping one meal won't kill you."

Instant rage, to the point that if she'd walked out of the bathroom right then, I might've eaten her face. Like, eaten her face *off*. Actually sunk my teeth in, grabbed and pulled skin until there was no face left.

"Stop being a pain," I hissed, slapping at the door and shaking the knob. "Get out of the bathroom!"

"Chill, you psycho."

"Oh, fuck you!"

"Girls?" Karen's voice drifted upstairs. "Do I need to come up there?"

"Only if you can get your daughter out of the shower so I can get to school on time," I snapped. "Or maybe you shouldn't 'cause she'll fucking poison me if she gets mad enough."

"What the hell, Emilia? I didn't do anything! Ugh."

"Quinn!" Karen stomped her way upstairs in her three-piece suit to pound on the door, her palm smacking against the wood so hard, she rattled the pictures on the wall. "You've had an hour. Let Emma in."

Quinn snorted. "Okay, Mom. Whatever. I'll come out when I'm done. Tell Tubby to wash in the sink downstairs if she's so worried about stinking. I'm so done with her bitchy ass."

I reared back like Quinn had struck me. My head swiveled Karen's way, my eyes so big, I thought they'd burst from the sockets. *How*, I wanted to ask. *How could you birth such a loathsome creature from your loins?* Karen couldn't hold my gaze. Her jaw clenched as she kicked the door, her sharp, pointed shoe striking over and over again.

"I'll break down the door, Quinn. Come out. *Now.*"

"Uh-huh. Sure you will, Mom. Why don't you go cry to your girlfriend about it? Tell her I poison my teammates for fun."

And then Quinn started to laugh, like my upset, her mother's upset, didn't register as anything other than droll inconveniences. She'd do what she wanted to do, there was nothing we could do about it, and if we didn't like it, *Oh, well.*

Karen glanced at me over her shoulder, some parts anger, desperation and embarrassment. My expression said it all. *Do something. Parent your kid.* But she couldn't enforce anything on her spoiled, horrible girl child.

"Don't grovel for the bathroom on my account. I'll skip my shower," I said quietly. Karen flinched, but my care cup was empty. I stormed back to my room and got dressed, so frustrated my eyes watered. I'd live without the shower, but it was the principle of the thing. Quinn was once again being a bully and getting away with it.

I was pulling on my jeans when there was a soft knock on my bedroom.

"Emma?"

Karen, again.

"What?"

"Can I come in?"

I didn't want her to, but there was no diplomatic way of saying no. I grumbled something incomprehensible that she must have taken as consent because she opened the door.

"I'm sorry. She's an angry girl. I'll switch with you going forward. You shower downstairs with your mother, and I'll come up here with Quinn."

"What's she got to be angry about?" I demanded. "What's so bad in her life that she's allowed to treat everyone like crap? She's got everything she could possibly need. She's pretty and thin and popular and she gets away with everything. Why's it so bad to be Quinn?"

Karen's mouth pinched. She wrapped her arms around her middle as if to give herself a hug. "I'm not making excuses. She's been angry since the divorce. She wasn't always like this. She got more difficult after the divorce, but it wasn't…" She paused to gesture over her shoulder. "To this degree. She prefers Alan."

"Then he should suck it up and let her stay with him. The kid came before the new wife."

"He doesn't want her," Karen blurted. The moment it escaped her lips, she swept her hand over her mouth, looking guilty. “I shouldn’t say that. He loves her, but I don’t think he wants to…deal. With her.”

“No one does.” I squeezed past Karen to head downstairs, shaking my head. Quinn was still in the bathroom, but she’d since turned on the radio to drown out her dissenters. I glanced at the clock. I had enough time to scarf a Pop-Tart before I had to hit the bus.

Karen followed me into the kitchen. When I tried to reach for the Pop-Tart, she cut me off, grabbing one for me like this would make amends. I eyeballed her, stuffing the toaster pastry into my mouth. I had just crammed the second into my face when Princess made her appearance. She ran downstairs looking like a Gilligan’s Island castaway. Coconut-shell bra. Short straw skirt. Sandals. A flower in her hair. The zit that had caused her so much distress was nonexistent on that perfect body as far as I could see.

“What’s all this?” Karen demanded. “You can’t go to school like that. Go change.”

“Yes, I can. It’s for prom committee. The cheerleaders are rallying for a luau theme and we all agreed to dress up. Don’t suck, Mom.” She stomped her way to the fridge. “Move,” she snapped at me. I didn’t get out of the way fast enough for her liking. When she jerked open the door, it smacked against my hip, hard. I slapped my hand over what would be a heck of a bruise in the morning.

“Are you done?” I hissed, “Seriously?”

“I have no idea what you’re talking about, *Emilia*.”

She smiled sweetly and sipped her water.

The casual dismissal was the last straw.

CHAPTER TWENTY-FOUR

I WHIPPED THE POP-TART AT HER HEAD AS HARD AS I could. It struck her on the side of the face, which was surprising because it was the first and last time I had good aim in my life. She squawked, a smear of blue frosting and rainbow sprinkles soiling her cheek, her water dropping to the floor.

"I HATE YOU!" I screamed. I reached behind me and grabbed the paper towels, throwing those, as well. Quinn screeched and lunged for me, her hand swiping out to grab a fistful of my hair. Karen shouted, getting in between us as Quinn and I swore and kicked and clawed. We'd fought many-a-time since moving in together but never physically. The only thing keeping us from shredding one another to pieces was Karen, and then my mother, who swooped into the kitchen from the bathroom, a towel on her head, a bathrobe hugging her body.

"What's going on?" Seeing Karen sandwiched between me and Quinn, Mom grabbed Quinn and hauled her back, her arms around her middle. Quinn turned around and slapped my mom across the face. I've never seen anyone react so fast in my life. My mother grabbed Quinn and shoved her against the wall, pinning her shoulders with her hands. When Quinn thrashed, my mother shoved her against the wall again, using her superior weight to hold her in place.

Mom's eyebrow twitched, her cheek pink from where Quinn struck her.

"You will not touch me again."

"Whatever," Quinn said. "Tell your cunt daughter to keep her hands to herself!"

Mom shook Quinn so hard, Quinn's head thwacked into the wall. I'd never seen that look on my mother's face before, and I never wanted to again. Her eyes were rimmed red, her lips pulled back to expose her teeth like a snarling she-bear.

"You will *never* use that word in my presence again."

Quinn opened her mouth to speak again, but my mother gave her shoulders one last shove, silencing any protests.

"It's not Emma's fault," Karen said, her voice meek. "Quinn provoked her." Karen ran her hands down my biceps and gave me a gentle squeeze. Her suit was disheveled, her hair no longer in the neat bun it had been moments ago. Blond hair stuck out from the sides of her head in tufts, and there were scratches along her neck that I was pretty sure I wasn't responsible for, but everything had been such a blur I couldn't be certain.

"I did not! She threw her Pop-Tart at me. What is wrong with you, Mom?"

Before my mother could shake Quinn again, before Karen could intervene, I unleashed. All of the hatred and Quinn-born insecurities became a torrent of hateful words I had to expunge before they rotted my guts out from the inside.

"No, what's wrong with *you*? I can't stand you. My mother can't stand you. Your mother barely tolerates you. You're a loser. A skinny, pretty loser who'll be assembling number sixes with extra cheese the rest of your life because you're too stupid to do anything else. I'll be sure to send you postcards from Cornell."

I knew I'd gotten to her when her face went from angry pink to purple. Her eyes welled with tears as she broke away from my mother to retreat into the hall.

"I hope all of you *fucking die*. I'm calling Daddy."

As she reached for her cell phone, I dealt the final blow.

"What? So he can tell you that he's sorry, but he can't take you in right now? That it didn't go so well last time, Princess? Surprise, asshole, he doesn't want you, either. How's it feel to know that your own parents can't stand you?"

"Emma," my mother chided, but it was quiet, almost too soft to hear. Karen covered her mouth with her hand to stifle a moan. Quinn looked between all of us, let out a muffled shriek and ran past us to flee outside. I said nothing as I grabbed my book bag and headed to the bus stop. I could hear Quinn screaming inside the garage. There was a crash and a litany of swears followed by the sound of breaking glass.

My science project. I'll have to start over.

God, I hate her.

I practically ran to the end of the street, tears threatening to erupt but never quite surfacing. I expected one of the mothers to follow me, at the very least to ensure I hadn't stopped to beat Quinn to death with my shoe, but no one surfaced. I got on the bus and checked my phone. No messages. Not on the ride. Not during my first class. Not during my second, either. It was disconcerting considering my moms' track records during times of duress. They always checked on me, always ensured I was okay.

That they hadn't meant something, I just wasn't sure what.

I was still fretting about it when the lunch bell rang. Shawn sat on my right, Nikki across from me, Laney and Tommy beside her on the end. Justice wasn't there but then, how could anyone blame her?

"How is she?" I asked Nikki.

She shrugged. "Not good, but that's to be expected. They're taking her to the doctor later." I hadn't mentioned the ex-lax or the shakes yet. Nikki had been busy taking care of her not-girlfriend-but-totally-her-girlfriend all weekend and I didn't want to burden her. Getting Justice healthy was the most important thing.

There was also the part of me that hoped Nikki would come to me with an accusation so I didn't once again have to be a whistle-blower on my own stepsister.

Except.

"She's got Crohn's disease and celiac disease and it's a really bad mix. They went out to eat the night before, and the restaurant served her something with wheat flour. Her mom called and they apologized, but like, what good does that do? They're looking at suing for emotional distress. Her mom's really mad."

Shawn side-eyed me.

I shifted in my seat.

Oh, no.

"She looked fine when I saw her in the locker room Saturday," I said.

Nikki nodded. "It comes on really quick. We had to leave the movies once because of it. It sucks. They're looking at a surgery to take out some of her lower intestine. You don't mess around with Crohn's."

Shit, shit, shit.

What if Quinn didn't do it?

I must have been wearing A Face because Nikki tilted her head. "What? You okay?"

"I thought it might be the shakes. The diet shakes. She was drinking one," I said carefully.

"Oh. Nah, she's been on those awhile. She had one before the competition but she couldn't finish it because her stomach went to rot. They're pretty sure it's the meal the night before. Food takes at least a day to go through your system."

You saw Justice open that can. Quinn couldn't have tampered with it.

Unless Justice put it down somewhere and Quinn drugged it between sips. But twenty-four hours…

Hell.

I closed my eyes. "I thought Quinn did something to her. I even… I didn't accuse her, but I may as well have. Crap. I'm going to have to apologize."

"Huh? Oh, no. This is…it sucks, but this is all Justice's condition. I hope the kids at school aren't awful about it." Nikki smirked. "For once we can't blame Quinn."

But I did blame Quinn. That's the problem.

"Anyone who says anything to Justice about it is an asshole," Laney said. "But, like, they'll get over it eventually. They always do."

Tommy nodded. "Yeah. She can hang with us. I won't bring it up. I feel sorry for her."

Nikki managed a smile. "Thanks, guys."

I felt like the world's biggest screwup. I'd said some hideous stuff to Quinn during the argument. She'd been annoying all morning, but she was probably pissed off I'd insinuated she'd drugged Justice in the first place. Anyone in her position would have copped attitude.

I screwed the pooch on this one. Hard.

Shawn must have sensed my guilt spiral as he leaned in close to me, his chin on my shoulder so he could whisper in my ear.

"Chin up, Superman. Apologize and it'll be fine. She'll get over it. It's not like she's not capable of doing something like that. There's no way you could have known."

"Yeah, I guess."

I poked at my lunch tray but I wasn't very hungry. I was spared the "do I eat the brick of pizza or don't I" decision when Mr. Malinski rushed into the lunchroom. He surveyed the crowd, talked to one of the on-duty monitors, and then hurried to our table in the corner.

"Emma? Your mother's here. Come to the office, please?"

Something's wrong.

"What's going on?" Shawn asked.

"I don't know," I said. Mr. Malinski wasn't talking.

"I'll text you later." I grabbed my book bag and followed Mr. Malinski out of the cafeteria. My friends called encouragement at my back as I crested the hall. I had no idea what to expect going into the office—Mommy rage, maybe, for the fight. Except the moment I saw my mother's face, I knew it was bigger than that. She looked haggard. Deep bags under her eyes. A pink tinge to her nose. A frown that could have curdled milk.

"I messed up," I said right off the bat. "I judged her and I..."

"It's fine. We have to go, okay? Do you need to go to your locker?"

"I didn't mean to make anyone's life hard. I...no, I can bring this stuff home for homework." Mom looked so upset, and my mind immediately skipped to a breakup with Karen in the wake of the fight. Clashing daughters, moms having to pick their own kids, a separation *for the good of the families.* "I'll talk to Karen," I added as we headed for the parking lot. "I can fix it. We'll work it out. I was an asshole."

"Emma, no. I..."

"I'm so sorry."

"Emma!" My mom grabbed me by the shoulders and spun me until we were face-to-face, putting me within an inch of that strain-riddled face. "No one cares about the fight. Quinn's dead." She paused and sucked in a breath. "She died. In the garage."

CHAPTER TWENTY-FIVE

LEAVING CAMPUS WAS A BLUR. MOM THROTTLED THE steering wheel like she wanted to strangle it. I peered out the window at the passing scenery, my fingers worrying the nylon loop on the top of my book bag.

"She didn't carry her EpiPen," Mom said as she turned the car onto the main road bisecting our town. "Karen always told her to carry it but she never did. Three minutes, the doctor at the hospital said. That's all it takes for bad allergies. We were inside talking. Karen went to check on her but it was already too late. She was facedown, ass up… it was so undignified, Emma. I can't… It was awful."

"What did it?" I asked quietly.

"Hornets. She had three stings and…we were inside. Didn't hear her. By the time we got out there she was gone. Fifteen minutes. That was it." Mom swallowed hard, tears dribbling down her cheeks.

I got stung this weekend. I should have said something.

The shock left me numb. I clenched my eyes shut, squeezing to see if this was a dream or a freakish reality where Quinn really was forever gone. There was no waking, only emptiness with a storm of emotion brewing on the horizon. I'd feel something, but not yet. My mind and body weren't ready yet.

"Who's with Karen?"

"Alan. He brought her back from the hospital while I got you. I have to make calls. She can't. She's devastated."

I nodded. I couldn't manage anything else.

Radio silence as we pulled into the driveway. I was halfway up the front steps when I heard the crying. Karen shrieked, Alan trying to comfort her with soft, crooning words. Mom put her hand on my back and pushed me forward despite my instincts telling me to stay away from such horrible pain.

The moment I crossed inside, Karen rose from the table to pull me into a bear hug. Long hair. Perfumed neck. Clinging arms. Mom hugged me from behind. I was sandwiched, struggling not to drown in their ocean of tears. I wasn't ready to cry—or maybe I wasn't willing, not for a girl who'd been the bane of my existence until four hours ago. But you can't be surrounded by that much sad without a modicum of transference. My head swam. My stomach lurched. The morning's Pop-Tart became a torpedo aimed at my throat and only long, deep breaths kept me from upchucking down the back of Karen's blouse.

The hugfest continued, Alan a silent, looming presence somewhere to my right. I wasn't sure the moms would ever let me go, but then the phone rang. And rang. It rang damn near incessantly after word got out that Quinn died. Alan put on the coffeemaker while my mother fielded the calls.

I got a look at Alan's face when Karen finally released me. His eyes were as red as his skin, his bottom lip quivering.

I escaped to my room, my emotions so tangled I didn't know which way was up. Quinn had spent the better part of our time together torturing me with daily affirmations like *If you dress like that, you'll be the lonely old lady who smells like cat pee*. The nastiness convoluted any grief I may or may not have had for her.

But, oh, how I pitied the wailing mother downstairs. She was in ruins, wrestling not just the tragedy of losing her only kid but guilt, too. Guilt that there was a fight. Guilt that her last interaction with Quinn was a scolding. I understood those feelings all too well. I'd pinned Justice's problems on Quinn and gotten her in trouble. I'd said terrible things. I never mentioned the hornets. I didn't know Quinn was allergic to them, but she was allergic to a whole heck of a lot of other stuff, so I should have assumed.

And now she's dead.

I dived into my bed and pulled up the pillows so they drowned out the weeping. I wanted to mute the world while I reconciled the craziest thing that had ever happened to me, but then my cell phone buzzed inside my pocket. I almost ignored it, but then it buzzed again and again, like a nest of angry bees…

Bees. Bees killed her.

Holy crap.

…against my hip. I fished it out, intending to turn it off, but then I saw Shawn's name at the top of a text.

You okay over there? he asked.

Quinn's dead, I typed back, then stared at the words for long minutes before pushing Send.

Are you serious?

She got stung by a hornet and she died. It's so messed up.

Holy crap. Let me know if there's anything I can do. So sorry.

I didn't answer, not him, not Nikki, Laney, or Tommy when they texted me. I ignored the barrage as word floated from my friends to everyone else in the school. Snapchat would be a mess later. Twitter and Yik Yak, too. People who'd never bothered with me were going to bother with me because my stepsister, one of our classmates, a girl everyone loved to hate and hated to love, had passed away.

Condolences, RIPs and questions poured in, a tidal wave of concern and morbid curiosity. I had no energy for anyone except Melody. Melody and Quinn had been friends almost since the beginning. There'd been spats, but they'd always resolved them to stand side by side at the top of the world.

Is it true? Melody wrote.

Yes. I'm sorry.

OMG.

Oh my God, indeed.

Self-defense sleeping is a time-honored technique of Not Dealing with It and a personal favorite. Have a noxious case of the Dunwannas? Dive under a comforter and pretend responsibility is a thing for other humans. School got you down? Nap until the craps have fled the crap farm. Have a raging swampbeast stepsister who tells everyone about your post-gym pit stains? Hit the mattress and hope she's eaten by crocodiles in your dreams.

Have the same stepsister die unexpectedly on a Monday morning?

Sleep avoidance is a go!

I'd managed an hour of doze time. Drooling into my pillow was far less complicated than sorting my sort-of-but-not-really sad feelings. Unfortunately, at suppertime, I was forced awake by the frenzied barking of Versace. I crawled from my blankets and stumbled toward the ruckus only to discover that he'd managed to get himself locked in Quinn's room.

...and I'd have to open the door to let him out.

I hesitated. It felt wrong to go into her room. *Too soon,* my brain screamed. *Too soon.* But what choice did I have? The dog was in there. My fingers grazed the doorknob and my body tensed. It wasn't sadness, but fear, like I could somehow contract Quinn's mortality by entering her sanctum posthumously.

Seventeen-year-olds aren't supposed to die.

I forced myself in. Everything looked exactly how she'd left it: makeup strewed across the counter, clothes on the floor, shoes piled in a heap save for a single pair. Prada, she told me once, when I asked her why she liked them so much, like that was a reason to like something—its designer label.

I peered at them stupidly. They'd been Karen's gift to Quinn when they fought about Quinn blowing past curfew three weekends in a row. Karen told Quinn she needed to do better, Quinn screamed that Karen put too much pressure on her, Karen bought her shoes to calm her down.

I reached for a sandal and sat on the corner of the bed. I

didn't want to scoot back into the nest of pink sheets and white blankets. It felt irreverent, like I was soiling sacred space. I turned the shoe over, fingering the fine straps of leather that crisscrossed around the ankles and the big, chunky heel with the basket weave glued to the frame. They were impractical shoes, but Quinn had looked good in them when she wore them. She'd looked good in everything.

My gaze drifted to her closet. It was the only part of her room that was organized. The shirts were on hangers on the top, the skirts on the bottom left, slacks and jeans stacked neatly on the right. Holding that shoe, looking at all those clothes, I couldn't help but think how sad it was that *this* was what I'd remember most about my stepsister. Her unbelievable wardrobe.

Versace let out a soft chuff to my left. I glanced at him. He licked his chops and barked before spinning in an excited circle. I was ignoring him, after all, and this was unacceptable to a wee Chihuahua brain.

"What?"

He sat on the ground and wagged.

"Y-you can have them if you want." I hadn't heard Karen approach. She stood in the doorway in a navy blue bathrobe with swollen eyes and a puffy face. Her fingers danced along the fringe at the cuffs, tugging and straightening and snapping, possibly in an effort to hide how badly her hands trembled.

I immediately stood from Quinn's bed, dropping the shoe like I'd been caught pillaging. "No, no. I'm sorry. I was just getting the dog. The shoe was in the middle of the floor so I… Sorry."

I started for the door but Karen put up her hand to stop

me. A chunk of hair fell into her eyes but she didn't bat it away. "It's okay. Take the shoes. You'd look nice in them. You're both nines. It's better they go to use. I'll just give it all away wh-whe..." She couldn't finish her sentence, the lump in her throat choking her words. She peered at me and then at the room, her shoulders hunching. "Anyway, take what you'd like."

"I don't think Quinn would appreciate me touching her stuff," I said quietly. "We didn't part on the best terms."

Karen sniffed, rubbing her sleeve along the underside of her nose. "The material stuff doesn't matter. Not anymore. Take what you want, Emma. You deserve nice things."

CHAPTER TWENTY-SIX

THE PRADA SAT ON THE CORNER OF MY DESK, BUCKLES gleaming gold under the ceiling light. I stared at them, contemplating all matters Quinn Littleton, when my cell phone vibrated. Nikki, live and actual.

"Are you going to the vigil tomorrow night?" she said in greeting.

"What vigil?"

"Ahadi called school for the rest of the week. There's a candlelight vigil tomorrow for the students. I wasn't sure if your family was coming."

As I'd heard nothing about it until Nikki's call, I wasn't sure, either.

"I'll get back to you. I have no idea what's going on. I doubt they even know about it."

"I'll come get you if you need me to. Like, if your family doesn't want to go but you do. I'm going either way."

I sucked in a breath. The Quinn/Nikki rivalry was no secret, and if I had to make a Top Ten List of people who'd gleefully prance over Quinn's corpse, Nikki damn near topped it. "Why? I mean, it's cool, I just don't want you doing something that'd make you uncomfortable for my sake."

"It's the right thing to do when someone dies? So, I'm going. Text me when you know what's up and if you need any help."

"Will do. Thanks, babe."

"No prob. Give my condolences to your family."

I headed downstairs, the cell clasped in my palm. Mom stood alone in front of the dishwasher, her hands supporting her lower back, her eyes closed. Her face pointed at the ceiling. I could see the strain there—the pinch of her lips, the lines creasing her brow.

She's worried about Karen.

I never had the sense Mom particularly liked Quinn. Their interactions were measured, especially when Quinn went full Bitchzilla-on-Tokyo mode. Mom would leave the room or find something to preoccupy herself with so she didn't verbally eviscerate her stepdaughter. It wasn't until recently that Mom started speaking her mind—only after I filled Mom in on some of Quinn's more discreet abuses.

I wondered if she regretted it now, with Quinn gone.

I eased into the kitchen. "Hey. How are you doing?"

Mom's demeanor softened. She opened her arms in invitation. "As well as can be expected. C'mere." I stepped into the hug knowing I'd be seeing a lot more like it in the future. Contact was reassurance. One girl was gone, but one remained. I was an anchor against the battering storm. "Keep your voice down. Karen took a sedative after Alan left. She's fitful, but some sleep is better than no sleep." Mom's lips grazed my forehead. "How are you holding up?"

"Okay, I guess. I feel bad for Karen."

Her arms tightened around my middle. "I do, too. I don't know what I'd do. If I was her—losing a daughter."

Mom fussed over me, tugging on my T-shirt, toying with my hair. I endured the ministrations partly because she had me trapped, but mostly because I knew it made her feel better. My chin settled on her shoulder. "Nikki called. There's a vigil at the school tomorrow. I don't know if anyone told you about it."

Mom paused, the furrows in her brow reappearing as she looked up in the direction of her bedroom and the sleeping Karen. "I don't know that she'd be up for that. It's a nice sentiment, but she's not ready for people. They'll understand. Or, they should. Shit."

Mom looked stressed. I had no burning desire to go myself, but I could see the merit in someone from the house making an appearance. It was a token gesture, but one I could stomach especially knowing Nikki would be there as a buffer.

"I'll go, if you want. Nikki offered to take me."

"Are you sure?" Mom rubbed her eyes with the butts of her palms. "I don't want you swarmed by busybodies."

"I'll be okay. I'll just say 'No comment' or whatever it is politicians do when they're caught porking their secretaries."

A ghost of a smile played around Mom's mouth. I managed to escape hug range while she was momentarily distracted. "I'll get the details from Nikki. I'm betting Nikki's dad will be around if it's a big community outing—the police will be there. He wouldn't let anything happen to me."

Mom nodded. "I like Officer Lambert. If you want to go, you can. If not, there's no pressure from me. Us. It's up to you."

"Okay."

Want didn't factor into it so much as someone had to mop up all the pseudo-condolences and mock sympathy. Quinn would roll her eyes that it was me, but what choice was there?

I texted Nikki on the way back to my room.

I'll go. Karen's in no condition and Mom's got to sit with her. You're sure this is okay?

Yes. Pick you up tomorrow.

Karen's mood rode a wave throughout the night; sometimes it was silent calm, other times heartrending misery. At one point she screamed and something crashed and broke in the foyer, like she'd thrown a dish or shattered a picture frame. I heard my mother consoling her, trying to bring peace, and I wanted to help, but how?

The time to help Karen was before, when Quinn was still here. When you could have not driven her outside. When you could have warned her about the hornets. When you could have…

Stop.

Brain, stop!

My stomach hurt. I curled in bed with Versace, my blankets down-filled Kevlar against the world. He snuggled close to my chest, content with his role as my living teddy bear. His face settled in the valley between my boobs. I had no idea how he could breathe, but he seemed happy, so I left him there to suffocate if that's how he chose to go.

My hand crept out from my safety cavern to reach for the phone on the end table. Firing it up brought too many people too close—people I'd never talked to, people who'd made fun of me for years, people who'd nodded at me twice total in their entire lives—and I promptly shut it down, overwhelmed. I wanted to talk to Shawn, but not at the expense of my sanity. Every ding or vibration was another reminder of the thing I was valiantly trying to escape.

This doesn't feel real. How is this even real?

Early to sleep meant early to rise. I was up at seven, before the moms. The inside of the house was silent. The outside was a spring-fueled playground with a thousand squawking birds. I padded downstairs, careful to avoid the pieces of shattered vase from Karen's outburst. A hop, skip and jump later and I was in the kitchen, grabbing a yogurt and some juice before scurrying back to my nerd cave.

I hunkered down in my computer chair, not really tasting my breakfast so much as shoveling it blindly into my face hole because sustenance was good for living. Versace stared at me, enthralled, so I shared the empty carton with him, watching him dive at it, nose buried in the plastic cup. Quinn's shoes lingered on the corner of my desk. I stroked the gold lamé interior from toes to arch, my fingernail worrying at the stitched-in label.

"I'm sorry you died," I said to Quinn via Prada. Strange, probably, but appropriate in a way, too. Quinn had been closer to this footwear than she was to most humans. Her beloveds were hunks of dead cow stretched over plastic-and-metal frames.

I picked up the left shoe, letting it dangle from my finger by the strap. "Take them," Karen had said and I'd taken them. I slipped it on. A perfect fit—Cinderella at the dead girl's ball. I donned the other and stood from my computer chair. I was a sneaker wearer most days and these were two-and-a-half-inch heels. I tottered around my room feeling like a phony. Quinn and I wore the same size, but she had made these sandals glamorous. They extended her legs. They made her toes look cute.

The chasm between her and me had never felt more tremendous. I didn't take care of my feet. Quinn said as much just last month, when the warmer weather settled in. *Get a pedicure, Lizard Girl,* she'd snorted derisively at my uneven toenails and ugly callouses.

Seeing my unkempt feet in the beautiful, too-expensive sandals, I wanted that pedicure more than anything in the world. It didn't make a lot of sense. It wasn't like I would understand Quinn better if I took after her, only maybe it did? Maybe we'd connect in a way we never had in life?

I have no idea what I'm doing.

I took off the shoes and sprawled back in bed to stare at the ceiling. By the time I got dressed and ventured downstairs, the moms had surfaced. They sat around in their pajamas, grilled cheese sandwiches plated before them. Karen's wasn't touched. She forced a smile for my sake, crooking a finger at me to motion me close. I sidled up beside her. She looped an arm around my waist, pressing a warm kiss to my upper arm.

"Hey, sweetheart. What are you up to?"

"I want to get my feet done before the vigil tonight." Both of my moms peered at me and then at each other, like their reasonable daughter had mutated before their eyes. "I know it's weird. But Karen gave me a nice pair of shoes and I want to look less like a lizard girl wearing them." My voice cracked, the joke falling flat.

"Now? You want to go now?" my mother asked. "Don't you think it's a little soon to—"

"It's okay, Dana. I'm no fun to be around, I know." Karen stroked my hair before reaching for her purse, fishing out two fresh twenties and laying them in my palm. "And it's a little bit of therapy, isn't it? Pampering ourselves. Maybe I'll do it after…well. After." Her eye twitched and she jerked her gaze away from me.

I glanced at Mom. "If you're not cool with it, I can stay."

"No, no. It's fine. Do you want a ride?"

"Nah. You stay here and take care of Karen. I'll walk. I shouldn't be long." I headed for the door, my hand freezing on the slider. "Thanks for the money, Karen. I appreciate it."

Karen's eyes welled with tears. Her lips pursed as she twined her fingers with my mom's. She didn't say anything, just nodded, and I took that as my cue to duck out into the warm spring day.

CHAPTER TWENTY-SEVEN

MY FIRST PEDICURE WAS NOT THE RELAXING SPA experience I'd hoped for. I expected cucumber slices and mud scrubs. It more resembled dungeon torture with its near boiling water, hot wax and metal files for my calluses. The lady worked my feet so hard, I expected to see nothing but bone below my ankles.

By the time the pink polish came into the picture, I clutched the armrests of the chair in terror. But when she was done? My size-nine ski feet were cute, soft and scale-free. I walked back to the house with my head down so I could admire the way the sun struck the lacquer. They were, for the first and only time in my life, adequate to fill Quinn Littleton's shoes.

Now my shoes, if I want.

But do I want?

The spring day was perfect with its blue sky and fluffy clouds and blooming green foliage. It was so at odds with the gloomy reality of Quinn's death. Standing outside my house, I eyed the garage. It had seemed so innocuous yesterday—a place for cars, lawn mowers and science projects. Today, it had gravity. It was, and forever would be, The Place Quinn Died.

I winced and walked into the house.

My mother was in the kitchen, the phone glued to her ear. A snore from the living room told me Karen had succumbed to sleep. Mom "mmm-hmm'ed" into the portable while fishing around inside the refrigerator. A few seconds later, a bowl of Saran Wrap–covered salad appeared in her hand. She shoved it at me.

"I'm on the phone with Grandma," she whispered. "Alan called. The wake is tomorrow, two viewings. One and six. The funeral is on Thursday. Do you need a dress?"

"Probably for the funeral, but I can go with Nikki or Shawn to get it."

"Okay, but if that doesn't pan out, let me know."

Mom stroked my brow and wandered toward her office to continue her one-sided conversation with my grandmother. I settled into a seat at the kitchen table, shoving the lettuce around inside the bowl awhile in hopes of finding an appetite. It didn't happen. I'd just crammed the bowl back into the fridge when a gray Honda Civic pulled into the driveway. Shawn. I rushed outside to head him off, not wanting him to accidentally wake Karen with a knock on the door. He climbed out, arms open, and pulled me in close to squeeze me.

"I got worried when I didn't hear from you. I brought you some pizzas from Papa Antonio's. Didn't figure anyone was much up for cooking, all things considered."

"That's… Thank you." I put my hands on his cheeks

and kissed him properly before sinking into the hug I didn't know I needed. His arms around my middle, his body touching mine. Heat to heat and it felt nice. "I can't believe she's gone," I said against his shoulder, muffled, my eyes fixed on the garage where she'd died.

"No one can. I'm so sorry. Are you holding up okay?"

"I think I am? I just feel bad." What I didn't say was that my guilt drowned me in a sea of *shoulda, woulda, couldas*. The hornets' nest. The false accusation about Justice. The fight and that awful finishing blow when I'd told Quinn no one wanted her, not even her parents. That was the hardest for me to reconcile—Quinn died thinking she was unloved. It wasn't true, but that hadn't mattered to me at the time. All I'd cared about was hurting her as much as she'd hurt me. It was a blow I couldn't take back, not now or ever.

I pinched my eyes shut. My eyes stung heavy with unshed tears, but even feeling as low as I did, my cheeks stayed dry.

I haven't cried for her yet. What's wrong with me? Am I that shallow?

"This sucks," I whimpered. "It really, really sucks."

Shawn perched his chin on my shoulder and held me close, his body rocking back and forth with mine. "I know, Superman. I know."

Shawn couldn't stay. With school closed, he'd taken an extra shift at Papa Antonio's but he promised to see me at the memorial service. I spent my day in quiet solitude, unless the Chihuahua counts, in which case I spent the day with my micro-dog. Karen woke from her nap at three, an outburst shortly thereafter sending my mother into damage-control mode. She ran her a bath. She served her tea and, when the crying threatened to float the house, a Xanax.

I stayed away. I was afraid to look Karen in the face. Afraid I'd see blame and loathing for my part in Quinn's death. It hadn't happened yet, but I wasn't convinced it wasn't coming nor was I convinced I didn't deserve it.

After a failed attempt at a slice of pizza that went back into the box with a single bite taken out of it, I got ready to go out. I'd seen Quinn wear her Pradas with slim-fitting jeans, so I did the same. I tended to hide beneath loose-fitting stuff, but Hufflepuff T-shirts weren't appropriate for the venue, especially considering Quinn used to make fun of me for *having a beaver on a shirt*. I'd tell her it was a badger, and that Tonks was awesome, but she never listened.

It doesn't matter if it's a badger or a beaver, Emilia. It's a furry weasel and you're wearing it. What is wrong with you?

A lot, Quinn. More than I ever knew.

And so it was that I delved back into Quinn's room to rifle through her dresser. Some of her smaller shirts wouldn't fit, especially not the ones that rode up and showed belly, but I grabbed a pale blue one that ran big on her but tight on me. I smoothed my hands down my sides, tugging at the bottom so it'd cover my belly flab.

What if the kids at school make fun of me?

...Suck it up if they do. This is about Quinn, not you.

God. Was I always so selfish?

I headed for the door, stumbling when I forgot about the wedges on the shoes. I steadied myself on Quinn's vanity, catching a glimpse of my reflection as I regained my footing. Glasses. Pale skin. A boring ponytail. I may have dressed Quinn's part, but I didn't look it. I brought my hair down, threading my fingers through the thick waves before reaching for her flat iron. Once, when she'd pretended to be my friend, she'd shown me how to use it. It was uncomfortable that the only time I'd get to put that knowledge to use was after she'd died.

Try not to think about that. Try not to think about anything.

It took twenty minutes from start to finish. Quinn used to make her prep look so easy and practiced, yet I stared at her makeup collection the same way Frodo looked at Mount Doom. Plastic tubes and colors had never been so intimidating. I swiped a mauve lip gloss from her kit and called it good, ducking into the bathroom and doing my best not to look at the basket of Quinn stuff beside the sink while I applied it.

It'll be cleaned out at some point. Sooner rather than later. I'm not sure if that's good or bad?

I'd just slid my phone, keys and the lip gloss into my pocket when Nikki beeped from the driveway. I eased my way downstairs. Mom was in the living room with Karen, Karen's head in her lap, her face turned toward the couch back. I wasn't sure if she was asleep or crying. Mom lifted her fingers in a silent wave. I returned the gesture and fled.

Nikki looked somber in the driver's seat. Her black slacks, white button-down shirt and understated makeup gave her an air of respectability, even with the slicked-back blue hair and lip ring. She was older Nikki, not party-fabulous Nikki, and I had the uncomfortable realization that everyone was probably going to age just a little bit because of the Quinn thing.

Death was a reality most teenagers never really considered until they had to.

"Hey," she said as I buckled myself in. "My dad's going to

meet us there. Justice had a late doctor's appointment but she'll be at the wake tomorrow. You look good."

"Thanks," I managed, but I didn't really feel like talking. She eyed me for a moment—my straight hair, borrowed shirt and shoes—but made no comment as she pulled us out of the driveway. We took familiar back roads to get to the high school. It should have been a ten-minute drive, but cars backed up all the way to North Main, which was a mile and a half out from campus.

Quinn commanded all this?

We waited in traffic awhile before Nikki brought out her phone. I didn't ask who she texted, but I wasn't left to wonder long. Blue lights flashed, a cop car coming at us from the opposite direction of the street. I expected Officer Lambert, but it was another cop I didn't know that pulled up beside us. He had white hair, a trim mustache and a wad of bubble gum stuffed into his cheek.

"Hi, Hal," Nikki said.

"Hey, kid. Follow me. Your dad reserved parking for you. Sorry for your loss, Miss MacLaren."

"Hey. Hi." It was weird that he knew my name and I didn't know his, but then, everyone in the universe probably knew about Quinn's demise. Westvale had never had a teenager die so young before.

Quinn was as much an anomaly in death as she'd been in life.

CHAPTER TWENTY-EIGHT

HUNDREDS OF PEOPLE GATHERED ON THE FOOTBALL field for the vigil, some seated on the bleachers, others milling around talking in small herds. The parking lot appeared full save for one plum spot in the front row that was blocked off by orange cones. We followed Hal's cruiser toward it, Nikki's father appearing as we neared to let us in.

Nikki goosed the gas to park *right* as a man walked in front of her bumper, forcing her to slam on her brakes. Standing in front of her car, looking stupefied that he'd been nearly splattered like road pizza, was a middle-aged man with a perpetual frown, a Santa Claus shape and a bald head so shiny he resembled Mr. Clean.

What was Mr. Riddell doing at Quinn's memorial vigil?

Nikki rolled down the window to stick her head outside. "Are you okay, Mr. Riddell?"

He looked baffled that she'd asked and even more baffled that two police officers ran at him while a car fender nudged his calf.

"Miss Lambert. Yes, I suppose I'm fine. I'm sorry. Are you all right?"

Considering he was the one who almost had to be scooped off the pavement with a spatula, it was nice of him to ask. Nikki nodded dumbly as her father and Hal cupped Mr. Riddell's elbows and eased him away from the parking spot.

"Damn, do you think he's here to do cartwheels?" Nikki asked. "Like, sing a chorus of 'Ding-Dong! The Witch Is Dead'?"

I looked down at my hands, the lump in my stomach no longer a pebble but a full-size boulder. "The time for that's long past. She's dead. You pay respects even when you don't like someone."

I wasn't unaware that I was spitting Nikki's own reasoning back at her.

I climbed from the car. My hands were everywhere—my shirt, my pants, my hair. I fussed like the pulls and tweaks would make me feel more comfortable in my skin. Nikki came to my side to loop her arm around my middle, half guiding me, half dragging me toward the milling bodies on the football field. For all that the mini-groups appeared haphazard, there was a pattern to it. They were planets orbiting a sun, the sun being a six-by-ten platform with three steps at the back and a podium at the center for Principal Ahadi to speak.

"Girls! Wait up!"

Officer Lambert. Nikki relinquished her hold on me so she could kiss her dad on the cheek. He rubbed her arm before nodding my way.

"Emma. Extend my condolences to your mother and

her—" he paused, unsure of what to call Karen. I almost took pity on him and said, "partner" but he smiled and lifted his hand to his face, fingers running down the sides of his mouth "—to your family for me?"

"Thanks. I will."

He gestured at the far side of the field, opposite of the road leading to the parking lot. A few white vans were parked near the tennis courts. "There's local press here. We've got an officer positioned to keep things under control. If you have a problem, I'll be standing next to the podium. Stick close."

"Thanks, Dad." Nikki dragged me off by my hand, navigating the throng to put us dead center to the podium, where everyone could see us. I had the terrible thought that the principal could pull me up on the platform during the vigil. What would I say if they asked me to speak? "Thanks for coming! When you think of Quinn, try not to remember how awful she could be. I'm sure if we collectively brainstorm, we'll come up with two or three things worth missing!"

I could point at the shoes maybe. Or the T-shirt I'd borrowed-slash-stolen. Or maybe the lovely mauve lipstick.

I bounced my weight from one foot to the other. The many sets of eyes pointed my way made me want to dive under the bleachers. Nikki touched the small of my back, probably so she could grab my T-shirt if I tried to escape. My hand swept over my brow, checking for sweat. None yet, but it was imminent if I didn't calm down, and wouldn't that be attractive.

"You'll be okay," she whispered. "I'm here."

"I shouldn't have come," I replied.

Pressure. So much pressure.

A hand brushed my elbow. I yelped and spun, so nervous I nearly jumped out of my skin, but it was only Laney and Tommy. They stood shoulder to shoulder, both of them holding unlit candles in conical paper guards. They were as muted as Nikki; Laney had dressed down in a plain black dress. Tommy wore slacks and a shirt with a skinny black tie.

The moment I looked Laney in the eye, she pulled me in for a hug, her arms squeezing so hard I thought she'd snap my spine. "How are you holding up? We're worried about you."

"I don't know how to answer that. I wish I did, but I don't." I pulled back and shook my head only to be dragged into a second embrace. My face pressed against Tommy's warm neck for a moment before he stepped away to haul Laney in close.

I shivered and it had nothing to do with the temperature. "I feel bad. We fought that morning and…I'm having a hard time." I didn't want to launch into another long-winded diatribe. It was self-indulgent when the focus should be not on Emma, the girl who didn't like Quinn, but the dead girl herself.

"Shawn said you were struggling. I'm so sorry. Is there anything I—we—can do?" Laney patted my hair like I was a beloved pet. I wanted to shoo her away but that required effort. "We'll be at both wakes tomorrow and the funeral on Thursday if you need anything."

"I need a dress for the funeral," I said. "Maybe we can all go out—I don't know when. The first wake's at one. There's no time. I should have gone today probably but I was hiding in my room."

"I have one you can borrow," Nikki said. "Don't sweat it."

I eyed Nikki's shape. She wasn't a small girl, but she wasn't quite my size, either. She was shorter. Trimmer through the waist. She nudged my foot with hers as if she knew exactly what I was thinking. "It's a little big on me, and it's stretchy. You'll look great."

"Okay, thanks."

I forced a smile right as my boyfriend pushed his way through the crowd. My smile transformed into something vaguely real. His head swiveled back and forth and I had to jump up to flag him down. Seeing me, he beelined my way, his hand outstretched. The press of his palm against mine quelled my nerves; he was yet another comfort in this little nest of comfort my friends had carved for me on the football field.

"Hey." He stepped into me, then around me, to hold me from behind, his arms wrapping around my waist. "You look nice."

"I'm wearing Quinn's shoes. Of course I do."

Every one of them looked down. Four sets of eyes regraded the Prada in much the same way I had earlier—they were extensions of the girl herself. A little bit of Quinn was there with us, her essence represented in strappy wedges, leather and shiny metal.

A gust of wind rippled across the field, kicking up my hair and blowing it across my face. I lifted my hand to the candle to protect the flame that burned for a girl that didn't inspire much in anyone except abject loathing. It was strange to be so careful with it when the whole vigil felt irreverent. I expected a few of Quinn's closer friends to cry or hold pictures of her to their hearts, but there was none of that. The cheerleaders flocked together, chattering quietly and sometimes laughing. Even Melody, Quinn's nearest and dearest, spent the entire time whispering to Josh or checking her phone. Once, I saw her dash at her face like there was a tear, but that could have been anything. Dust. A bug. An eyelash.

Josh smirked a lot, the prick.

Even the teachers seemed only quasi-invested. They dropped enough proper "such a shame"s that they could pass for polite, but they tended to look around a lot, disinterested in Principal Ahadi's speech. If they caught me looking at them, they'd lift their vigil candles at me, like toasting me with a drink, but then they'd quickly look away.

The only person there earnestly upset was Principal Ahadi. He wore his nice gray suit, the one with the lavender-and-silver tie that we saw whenever we had visitors to the high school. His hands grasped the edges of the podium like he needed them for support. His glasses were pushed down to the tip of his long nose, his bushy gray-black eyebrows low over his eyes. Every once in a while he read something from his pages and paused to clear his throat like he was overcome.

Which I didn't quite understand. Only I did a little and it went back to what Nikki and I both said: kids our age weren't supposed to die. Quinn was terrible, but given time and enough kicks in the teeth by the real world, maybe she could have settled into semi-functioning adulthood. But now she'd never have the opportunity to fulfill any secret potential lurking beneath the surface. And that sucked.

Ahadi stepped away from his perch, closing his tribute with a request for a moment of silence. Everyone was supposed to dip their heads and commune with whatever version of God they found most pleasing. We all looked at one another, shuffling our feet. More than a few people ogled me like they expected me to erupt into shrieking wails, but I was just as clueless as the rest of them about how to feel. Or grieve. Was I grieving? I didn't even know.

The threat of being called out for my dearth of warmth made me uncomfortable. Nikki and I had avoided attention when we'd arrived because of Mr. Riddell, her dad and then Ahadi taking the stage. There were no buffers left. I was the bug zapper and the people around me were mosquitoes out for blood.

I wanted away from the gawking horde of teachers, classmates, parents of classmates and townies as quick as possible. "Let's go. I'd rather not reenact *The Birds*."

"I've got her," Shawn said. "If that's cool, Nikki."

Nikki nodded. "Absolutely. Do you need the dress for tomorrow, Emma?"

"For Thursday. Just bring it to the wake."

"Will do. Love you, doll."

Laney swooped in for a cheek kiss and another hard hug. "See you tomorrow. If you need me, I'll have my phone on."

Tommy nodded. "Me, too. We're thinking of you and your family."

"Thanks, guys. I love you." I studied their faces. They were grave, unlike most people there, but it was strange in a way, too. None of them liked Quinn and yet…

It's for me. Even at Quinn's memorial service, the concern isn't for her but for me.

How? How is that possible?

I took Shawn's hand and headed off the football field, fleeing the hungry eyes of Westvale and my own tangled thoughts.

CHAPTER TWENTY-NINE

SHAWN WANTED TO SPEND SOME TIME TOGETHER BEFORE he dropped me off at home. We parked at Dairy Queen and shared a Banana Split Blizzard. It was vastly inferior to our regular hangout nights; there was no kissing or snuggling or whispered secrets, but it was a nice side venture during a week otherwise filled with death and mourning.

I stabbed my plastic spoon into the ice cream and wiped my face, smearing the napkin with mauve lip product in the process. "This whole thing is messed up."

"Yeah, it is." Shawn leaned forward to turn on the radio, immediately lowering the volume when it blared loud enough to shake the car. "She's the only young person I've ever known to die. My grandpa died but he was sick and old. This is really sudden."

"Maybe that's why no one seemed sad," I said. "Like, not even her friends. Maybe everyone's in shock." I glanced at Shawn's profile. "Can I say something to you and not have you think I'm being melodramatic or weird?"

"I never think that." He tilted his head back and smiled, shooting me eight trillion watts of gorgeous white teeth against gorgeous brown skin. "That's not really your thing. Being too hard on yourself is, but that's different."

I sucked in a long breath before speaking. "It's my fault."

Shawn's eyebrows lifted, his lips pursing like I'd suggested that Wednesdays should be called peanut butter and cows were green. "What? How?"

It poured out of me, a faucet of regret. How badly I felt about the accusation. How the fight had sent Quinn outside to the garage. How I'd been stung by a hornet not two days before and I never said anything.

"Hey. Hey now, Superman." Shawn's voice was quiet when he reached out to take my hand. "Okay, first off, did you know she had the allergy?"

"No…"

"Okay, so are you psychic?"

"…No."

"Right." He smiled faintly, his fingers threading through mine as he rested our joined hands on the car shift. "I can't let you shoulder any of this. And I'm not sure who would have given Quinn the benefit of the doubt with the Justice thing. Good faith is earned. Quinn didn't earn much of anything."

I managed a wobbly nod, my head swinging up and down like a bobblehead. He leaned over to kiss my cheek, his nose brushing my ear. "She was hard to get along with. It sucks that it was your last interaction with her, but man, if anyone could make another person lose it, it was Quinn. She had a talent for pissing people off."

"Maybe." I peered out the window at a flickering streetlamp

on the corner of the parking lot, trying to wrap my mind around the girl I'd lived with but never really knew. "I should have tried better to understand her. To figure out why she was the way she was. Before she died, I found a picture of her family, when Alan and Karen were still together. It was tucked away like she didn't want anyone to find it. The divorce messed her up. I always knew that, but the picture was confirmation, you know? I should have tried to help her then, but if I'm being real honest? I didn't want to. It was a lot of work for no guarantee of reward. Quinn was mean, and it was easier to call her a bitch and be done with her than to think about her much. Now that she's gone, I've got nothing but time to think about her, and I'm mad at myself for being so lazy."

Shawn sighed. "It's understandable, though. Her reasons for being a jerk mattered, sure, but I'm not sure they mattered so much she deserved a pass for being terrible to people."

"Of course not, but…okay, no one's born bad. I guess Hitler was, but Quinn wasn't Hitler. She could be an asshole, but I think she got there. She didn't start there." I took a moment to collect my thoughts. I didn't want to paint Quinn as something she wasn't—she was no saint and I'd never claim otherwise—but I also wanted to do something I'd never done when she was alive. I wanted to give her the benefit of the doubt.

Because, maybe, if people had done that more often, she wouldn't have been so difficult to get along with.

"She never got picked. Ever," I said. "I didn't really get that until the vigil. Everyone there that was legit upset was upset because they were friends with me, not because Quinn's gone. Even when she's dead, she's not the one people are thinking about."

Shawn listened but didn't say anything. I licked my lips.

"That picture of her as a kid. She looked happy and then one day she wasn't happy anymore. She blamed her mom for the divorce. The hostility… I'm guessing it had something to do with Karen being queer 'cause Quinn never really seemed okay with our moms being together. Hell, maybe messing around with Nikki was Quinn's way of trying to figure out what was up with her mom. Maybe she was trying to connect. It's a stretch, but not outside the realm of possibility."

Also not something I'll mention to Nikki. She's put the Quinn thing to rest. No point in opening up old wounds.

"What about her dad?" Shawn asked. "Why didn't she live with him?"

"I don't know for sure. I know he married a girl closer to Quinn's age than his own. Maybe the wife didn't want Quinn around? Which probably hurt because, once again, someone's picking other people over Quinn. And when Quinn and Karen moved in with us, Karen was super nice to me. She talked about college and helping me get into Cornell. But Quinn wasn't a great student, so she'd feel slighted and lash out. Karen bought her off to shut her up and nothing ever got resolved. It's like… God, Shawn. Even the dog picked me. Like, Quinn moved out for a couple months, came back, and when she came back Versace didn't stick with her. Who *wouldn't* be pissed off all the time?"

Shawn held his peace. I slumped into my seat to gaze up at the gray felt on the car ceiling. "I think all of us did what

Karen did to a degree. We gave Quinn enough lip service to keep her quiet and never bothered with her beyond that. We never looked past the screaming. I knew this on some level, back when I found that picture, and I didn't do anything about it, and I feel like a huge jerk."

"But you're not. It's tough to feel sorry for someone who's so vindictive. Like, look at what she did to Riddell," he said.

I shrugged. "Oh, I have, and it seems over-the-top until you consider he took her phone on a day her dad was supposed to call. He probably didn't realize what a big deal that was to her—I certainly didn't—but it was a big deal. Alan wasn't great at keeping in touch. Quinn valued that contact."

Shawn frowned. "That sucks. Still. If she'd been nicer to people, it would have made it easier to help her."

"You're right. It would have. But I'm not talking about what Quinn could have done to make people treat her better. I'm talking about what people could have done to treat Quinn better. There's a difference."

Shawn dropped me off with a kiss and a promise to see me the next day. My heels throbbed as I wobbled into the house. I kicked off the shoes into the pile in the corner of the kitchen, but the Prada looked too fancy to be among dingy sneakers and years-old flip-flops. I plucked them out and put them on the edge of the counter, sweeping an errant blade of grass off the tip of the right shoe.

"Put them on the stairs," Mom called from around the corner. "I just washed the counters."

"Do you have X-ray vision? You're not even in the room."

I relocated the shoes while Mom darted around the house like a bee at blossoms—cleaning the coffeemaker, rinsing dishes in the sink before putting them in the dishwasher, changing the bathroom trash. Her hair was in a sloppy ponytail, her T-shirt old and covered in paint splatters. She wore the pink pedal pushers she called her Fat Pants, which were reserved only for the direst of days.

"Why are you in a tizzy?" I asked.

"People will probably come over between wakes and I'd like it to be habitable."

She swooped in for a kiss—the bald eagle mama returning to the nest. Unlike the bald eagle mama, she didn't puke worms at me.

I plunked down at the table. Mom came to stand behind me, her pottery-strong hands massaging the muscles in my shoulders. It hurt, but I endured knowing it'd feel better later. My head lolled forward, hair falling away from my neck so she could rub along my spine.

"Where's Karen?"

"Upstairs. How was the vigil?"

"Fine, I guess. People stared at me."

"They'll do that." Mom tugged up my shirt and rolled it until it rested against my nape. Her hands worked down the bare skin of my back, around the straps of my bra. "It's the train wreck principle. No one really wants to see the mangled bodies and mangled steel, except everyone really wants to see the mangled bodies and mangled steel. Maybe to assure themselves they're still alive. It's morbid but typical."

"I wish they'd been sadder."

"They weren't?"

"No. Uncomfortable, maybe, but no one cried. Not even Melody. It made me sad for Quinn. She could be a pain but she deserves better than that." Mom didn't say anything as she pinched her way up my back, her fingers running into my hair to draw circles across my scalp. I closed my eyes, letting Mom knead my worries away. "I think everyone assumed she had everything so why would she need or want them around? Like, she was pretty and her family had money. People saw the privileges, not the girl beneath. It's hard to feel sorry for someone you never connect to beyond a bad, lingering first impression."

Mom's hands left my hair to clasp my shoulders, her chin resting atop my head. "You're pretty insightful, kid of mine."

"I wish I'd been this insightful sooner, when Quinn was still around for it to matter." I rubbed my face with my hands, weary of reality and its various Quinn-based gut punches. "I think I'm going to hit bed early. I'm exhausted."

"Okay. We need to be out of here tomorrow at noon for the wake. Oh, and I fed the dog. He was whining."

"Thanks. And I'll be ready."

A hug, a kiss, and I climbed the stairs, pausing to snag the Prada along the way. Quinn's door was open when I reached the landing. Karen sat in front of her daughter's dresser, piles of folded clothes surrounding her. I couldn't see her face, only the bun on top of her head and the pale column of her neck, but the ivory skin between ear and shoulder was splotched over with red hives.

"Hey, Karen. Are you okay?"

She obviously wasn't, but social contract required certain things of me. Asking how someone was even when you knew the answer was one such thing.

She motioned at Quinn's closet. "I dropped off Quinn's dress at the funeral home earlier. The pale blue one she liked so much. The Donna Karan." She sniffled and tilted her head to the side. "I almost picked the red one, but it wasn't designer label. She wouldn't have approved."

I didn't immediately reply because I didn't know *how* to reply, which prompted Karen's bark of harsh laughter. "It seems silly worrying about that now. I doubt the dead care about the trivial bullshit. Stuff. I shouldn't swear."

I moved aside one of the piles of folded clothes and plopped down beside her. She reached for my hand and pulled it into her lap, clinging to it like a lifeline. A few tears dribbled down her cheeks. She'd cried so hard at some point, she'd burst a blood vessel in her left eye. It was a red firework of color next to her blue iris.

My tendency to say something funny to break the tension reared its head. It would have been totally inappropriate to mention that the designer label was a good call because, in a zombie uprising, Quinn absolutely would have gone to the mall not to eat people but to hit Nordstrom's. Humor worked as a coping mechanism for me, but to other people, it could look like disrespect.

"She really liked that dress," I said instead. "It's a good pick."

Karen slumped her weight into my side. I leaned back against her, realizing for the first time it was less what I said to her that mattered and more that I was there—a human to fill the emptiness loss left behind. She snuggled in close, I snuggled back.

We were quiet awhile, both peering into the color-coordinated depths of a could-be fashion icon's closet. Occasionally, Karen sniffled.

"I've been sorting her clothes. The stack on the right has things that might fit you or I think you'd actually wear? Whatever you don't want I'll send to charity. I want you to take all the shoes and purses. And makeup. Take any of the skin care stuff, too. The rest of it I'll give away. I feel the need to be useful. Or, not to be useful, but—" Karen shuddered "—I want something good to come out of this. Anything good. Giving her stuff to people who need it, that feels like lemonade from lemons. I'm grasping, I know, but it all seems so senseless. I know she wasn't a peach, but there was time for her to turn it around. Seventeen's far too early to give up on anyone."

I squeezed Karen's hand again. "She was a green banana. Bananas don't get delicious until they're yellow."

"That's a good way to put it." Karen pressed a dry kiss to my cheek. "Can I ask a favor from you? If you don't want to, you don't have to, but your mom mentioned…well."

"Sure. Anything."

"Do you think you could do a reading tomorrow? You can pick it. I trust you. They have a folder of recommendations. Songs and bible passages and poems. I don't think I can get through it. Alan is doing one but…" Karen's voice cut off. She looked at me, nervous, like she was afraid I'd reject her. "I can ask your mom, too."

I thought about it for a minute before shaking my head. "No, it's cool. I'll do it."

"You're sure? You don't have to."

"I know I don't, but I'll do it."

Karen leaned in close to me, her arms around my waist, her face pressed to my shoulder. I squeezed her tight. She turned her face and sobbed into my hair.

CHAPTER THIRTY

FUNERAL READINGS SLANTED ONE OF THREE WAYS. Religious, which Quinn wasn't. Emotional, which too often focused on the sadness of the grievers instead of honoring the dead, and inspirational. Inspirational straddled the line; sometimes there were hints of spirituality, but most times it was a long, drawn-out version of one of those posters you saw in the doctor's office with mountains, a goat in harsh winds standing on a craggy cliff and the word *Achieve* printed beneath.

None of it captured what I wanted to say. Not that I was completely clear on what I wanted to say, but I figured I'd know it when I saw it, and I hadn't seen it yet.

For an hour I kept at the passages, some from the funeral home's website, some from the internet at large, but nothing moved me. I wanted it to be perfect. I *needed* it to be perfect. It was the last thing I could do to make amends to my stepsister. Karen had given me an opportunity to settle some of my debt and I wouldn't accept second best.

After yet another disappointing batch of poems, I wandered downstairs to find my mom. She was alone in front of the television, a bowl of microwave popcorn in her lap, ugly blue monster slippers on her feet.

"Hey. Is Karen asleep?"

"Yes, thank God. I had to drag her out of Quinn's room before she had another breakdown. She's not ready to unpack all of that yet. How are you doing?" She patted the couch beside her. I slid in, the leather sighing as my weight pushed the air from the cushion.

"Okay. She asked me to do a reading tomorrow. I don't like any of the ones I've found so far."

"Why not?" Mom offered me the popcorn but I declined. Food wasn't much of a priority when you felt sick all the time, and I felt pretty sick whenever I thought of Quinn. The ice cream from earlier was cold sludge in my gut.

"They don't suit her. I'm sure they work for other people, but not Quinn." I paused. "Do you think Karen would mind if I wrote my own?"

Mom looked at the television, her face belying nothing, which was, as per usual, a bad omen. "I'm not sure that's what Karen had in mind. I don't mean to be rude, but you didn't have the best relationship with Quinn."

Read between the lines, Emma.

"I'd never. I..." I sucked in a wheezy breath, expecting the tears to break, but still there was nothing. My voice was strangled when I talked, though, like some invisible shame monster was choking the life right out of me. "I wouldn't say anything bad about Quinn. I hope you know that. I know I said some awful stuff that morning, but I'd take it back if I could."

Mom's face fell. "Oh, honey. No. No. Come here." She pulled me close, forcing my head into the crook of her neck. Over the course of the days, Mom had become a walking, talking Kleenex for Karen. I wasn't at the breaking point yet, but it was close enough that she treated me like a most fragile thing. Her lips brushed across my forehead. "I'm not sure you knew her that well, that's all I meant. We all say things we don't mean when we're angry, and most times we get the opportunity to apologize. It didn't work out that way and it sucks. You know, Karen's in your position, too, and like I said to her, you have a choice to make. How do you want to remember Quinn? As fighting in the kitchen? Or as a vivacious girl who wasn't afraid to speak her mind?"

"The second," I conceded. "The first makes me feel like crap."

"Exactly. That's your guilt rearing its head, but you can't let it win or you'll be burdened by it the rest of your life. Hopefully, when the dust settles, we'll all be a little smarter for what happened. Maybe our takeaway can be that we don't part with people on bad terms going forward. We can prepare for a lot in life, but not everything. Fate's a fickle bitch like that."

"It's not fair," I said quietly.

"No, it's really not."

I settled in against my mom, closer to her than I'd been in a long, long time. I'd already thought about a lot of what she said—especially the part about choosing the dead's legacy. Often, after someone dies, they become far greater than they'd ever been in reality to the people left to mourn them. I'd considered that stupid, especially as it pertained to Quinn, but the more I thought about it, the more I realized what death did is put the petty differences in perspective. The things that had looked so monumental days ago looked insignificant through a different lens.

Quinn hadn't been nice to me, no, but I'd never been particularly nice to Quinn, either, and it wasn't always because she provoked me. I'd let past slights and petty annoyances steer our course.

The course led straight into the crapper.

"Do you still want to write it?" Mom asked, her voice muffled by my hair. "You can. I know you'll do your best."

"I think so, yeah. I think I know what I want to say now."

I worked for hours to get the wording right. By the time the draft was done, handwritten because it felt more personal than the computer, it was two in the morning and my fingers were cramping. I went to bed feeling like I'd accomplished what I'd set out to accomplish. It wasn't Native American prayers or Bob Dylan lyrics, but it was apt for the circumstances.

At least, that was my hope.

When my alarm sounded the next morning, Mom was on the phone nonstop and Karen was already gone. She and Alan had gone to the funeral home early, "to handle last-minute details," Mom said, but I knew what she meant. They'd gone for some privacy, before a trillion eyes witnessed their grief. I couldn't blame them for wanting alone time with their only daughter.

I dressed in proper garb—black pants. A lavender blouse with silky material that wasn't silk. Nylons and a good bra. I flattened my hair and wore the Prada, and even put on a little makeup and a pair of small, gold hoop earrings. Mom called for me at half past ten and I snagged the reading from my desk, weirdly numb to it all. I expected to be sad, or nervous about talking in front of people, but I couldn't muster much of anything except resignation that this was really a thing. I was off to Quinn's wake.

I passed her room, sparing a scratch for Versace, who wagged at me from his hallway rug perch, his ears tall and pointy and spinning in weird directions. Quinn's door was ajar, clothes stacked waist-high. The sheets and blankets were stripped from the bed, the mattress covered with dresses on hangers and other things Karen had pulled from the closet. The tops of the vanity and bureau were bare save for the cardboard boxes where Karen had put all of Quinn's miscellanea. Some clothes remained in the bureau still, in particular the lower registers. Looking at the rolled-up T-shirts in the bottom drawer, I remembered the Disney picture I'd found on her floor.

I'd put it in the bottom drawer when Quinn had moved out. I rifled through tank tops and bras just in case Quinn hadn't moved it. There, buried, was the picture, except it wasn't alone anymore. Quinn had put it in an envelope with the rest of her collection. All the photos were the same ilk—the Littletons before the split. Smiles. Happy faces. Christmas trees and presents and birthday parties with roller skates. There was one of Alan kissing Karen's cheek. There was one of Alan lifting a little Quinn up onto his shoulder. There was one of Karen holding an infant Quinn with one of those white puke rags over her chest.

I took the Disney one. While Karen wouldn't be able to stomach the rest of the pictures anytime soon, I recognized that one day, she might want them for nostalgia's sake. But

I'd decided the Disney one belonged to Quinn. I tucked it into my notebook and took the stairs two at a time to meet up with my mom. I heard her talking quietly, I thought to yet another someone on the phone, but when I turned the corner I saw her hovering in the doorway, whispering to my father.

He was in a navy blue suit, his brown hair slicked back, his face shaved bare outside of his graying mustache. He was tanner than I'd ever seen him, and the black-rimmed glasses sitting on his nose were new.

"Dad?"

He lifted his face to me, his smile stretching from one ear to the other. "Hey, sweetheart. Your mom called. I wanted to—"

I yelped before I hit his open arms. He held me close, murmuring quietly as he rocked me back and forth, practically picking me up off the floor in the process. My father is tall, six feet three inches, and broad across the shoulders. Mom used to joke he was shaped like a Maytag box. I was glad for his size then—for the safety it afforded me as I clung to him.

The detachment I'd felt, that emotional armor I'd woken up with, crumbled in his presence. I didn't cry, but I was young again, and scared, and vulnerable, and I'd never more felt like I'd understood Quinn than I did in that moment. I was seven, not seventeen, because my daddy was home.

CHAPTER THIRTY-ONE

WE ARRIVED A FULL HALF HOUR BEFORE THE FIRST viewing began. I'd never been to a funeral home before, and seeing the blue-and-white floral wallpaper, the beige industrial carpet and the white sofas with stiff backs and carved legs, I was all set with seeing one again. I'd have to, I knew, one day, but the place tried too hard to be welcoming. It wanted to appear homey when it was anything but. It had an odor. Not dead-person stink, but something chemically bland. A cleaner, maybe, or some of that powdery stuff you sprinkled onto the rugs to keep them fresh. I didn't like it. It gave me that same, uneasy feeling I got whenever I smelled the disinfected halls of the hospital.

There was an easel with a blown-up copy of Quinn's last professional picture from before Christmas. Karen and Alan spoke quietly with Alan's mother and new wife in front of it. Karen's face was pink and swollen. Alan's eyes were so red they looked like they were bleeding. Karen leaned on Alan like she couldn't stay upright without him. For this one thing, their differences were put aside; Alan supported Karen with one arm around her waist, the other under her elbow. She clutched his wrist, a handkerchief spilling over their joined fingers.

Mom and Dad signed a guest book near the front door before accompanying me into the room on the right. I didn't know what to call it beyond the casket room. The coffin was at the center of the back wall. A podium with a snakelike bendy microphone. Rows upon rows of chairs. A kneeling rail for prayers. Floral wreaths and bouquets covered the three side tables. Classical music played, something mellow and understated that couldn't possibly offend anyone. Kmart music, Mom would normally call it.

I was sandwiched between my parents as we approached the casket, my dad on the left, Mom on the right. I clasped my dad's hand like I needed it to not float away.

I wasn't ready for the girl in the box.

Quinn looked just like Quinn. She looked nothing like Quinn. Both. Neither. I couldn't decide. Her eyes were closed, her strawberry blonde hair fanned out on the silk pillow beneath her head. The makeup person had left her pale, which would have driven Quinn crazy—she used a lot of bronzer in the spring and summer because she'd go tanning and she wanted her face to match her body. The untouched white made her look delicate and china doll and *so very dead.* The too-red lips and sweeps of pink across her cheekbones did little to liven her up.

Mom and Dad let me go so I could kneel before the casket. I dropped my head and recovered a prayer from the darkest depths of my memory. I used to go to Sunday school. I knew some things even if they'd gone dusty with age. I could pray for someone going to Heaven and hope that the afterlife treated them well.

In Quinn's case, better than real life had. She wasn't a happy girl. Maybe there was peace on the other side.

I blessed myself and stood, peering at Quinn's too-still form. I remembered the picture in my notebook, and I pulled it out, giving it one last look before relinquishing it to the box. I slid it in near Quinn's shoulder so it rested against the pale pink lining. It'd go beneath the ground with her. A memento to last the ages. Happier times. Happier faces.

"I'm sorry," I whispered.

She didn't respond.

Looking down at her was so strange. My eyes played tricks on me. Sometimes it looked like she breathed, like her chest rose and fell, and I had to remind myself that no air had struck those lungs in days. Quinn had been prepared for these final hours topside with chemicals and paints and mystical coroner procedures.

Laney had made me watch *Six Feet Under* with her once. I wished I hadn't. Ignorance would have been kinder.

"Dana?"

Karen, from the door. She swept in to gather my mother up in her arms. They hugged, whispering quietly to one another.

"I didn't want to disturb you," I heard my mother say.

"You never do. Never."

My father looked away from both of them, focusing on the memorial wreaths.

"Emma wrote something for the service," Mom said. "Do you want to read it beforehand?"

I was tense as I stepped away from Quinn and her casket.

I turned, and Karen came toward me to pull me into the thousandth hug of two days. "No, no. I know my Emma. She'll do right. Thank you, sweetheart."

Her Emma.

A stand-in daughter.

I won't screw this up.

Shawn was the first of my contingent to arrive. I hadn't expected the whole Willis clan, but his parents accompanied him dressed in their funeral blacks. They nodded at me before taking seats in the middle of the room. I stood off to the side of the casket with my dad, out of the way. Karen and Mom greeted people with Alan by the front door. Shawn strode over to offer his hand to my father.

"Good to see you again, Mr. MacLaren," Shawn said.

"Shawn. Nice to see you. I'm sure Emma appreciates you coming." Dad patted his shoulder in that pseudo-awkward way parents do when greeting their teenager's significant other.

Shawn took it in stride. "How are you holding up, babe?"

My eyes strayed from the casket to the dozens of chairs in front of it and then to the window overlooking the parking lot. The spaces were filling fast, more cars lining up to turn in along the road. "I have to talk in front of people. Not good."

"You'll do fine. You're Superman, remember? You got this." He hugged me close, pressing yet another kiss to my ear before going to sit with his parents. The cheerleaders arrived next in flocks of three or four. Or maybe that was packs? Gaggles? Whatever the term, they sat in the back rows, black lumps of shocked faces and averted gazes. Some looked my way but most fixated on the coffin. The blasé attitudes from the school vigil were gone, replaced by muted horror. Seeing Quinn got to them in the same way it had gotten to me.

Everything was so much more serious with a corpse in the room.

The teachers came thereafter. Mr. Ahadi. Mr. Riddell, which surprised me considering the circumstances. Nikki arrived with her father and Justice at quarter of one. They sat in the third row, behind Quinn's family. Nikki beelined for me, crushing me to her in a fierce embrace, her eyeliner already smudging beneath her eyes. She kissed my cheek. I quietly thanked her and she returned to Justice's side, taking her hand and squeezing it in her lap.

Laney and Tommy sat in the fifth row with waves and solemn frowns. My grandmother took the second row with my aunts. Melody and Josh Winters. Half our junior class. The staff at Bouncing Bear minus Josh's dad. Mom ushered me to our front-row seats for the service as the room filled up.

And filled up.

And filled up.

It got ridiculous. No seats were left, standing room only, the people attending the wake and the ceremony spilling over into the main room and peering in through the open doorway. I didn't know half of them. Extended relatives of Quinn. Community figures. Friends of Alan and his new wife. It was overwhelming how many people were there and how many people continued to file in to celebrate a girl no one really knew all that well.

The minister took the podium. Reverend Lionel, he said. I didn't hear much of his sermon. There were Christian promises of ever-life in Heaven. Prayers. A few anecdotes Karen must have shared from Quinn's childhood. I couldn't stop looking at Quinn in her casket, wishing I'd had Monday to do over again. Wishing I could change just two or three things to make it all better.

For more than a year I'd begged God to make Quinn go away. He'd answered me and now I was begging Him to give her back, for Karen's and Alan's sakes, but that wasn't how it worked.

Alan took to the podium to do his reading, pulling a small pair of glasses from his coat pocket. He eyed the enormous crowd, then the paper and cleared his throat. His fingers tapped on the edges of the wood, his feet shuffled as he began to speak. Within one line I knew it was from *The Tempest*, which we'd studied the year before.

"Be cheerful, sir.
Our revels now are ended. These our actors,
As I foretold you, were all spirits and
Are melted into air, into thin air:
And, like the baseless fabric of this vision,
The cloud-capp'd towers, the gorgeous palaces,
The solemn temples, the great globe itself,
Yea, all which it inherit, shall dissolve
And, like this insubstantial pageant faded,
Leave not a rack behind. We are such stuff
As dreams are made on, and our little life
Is rounded with a sleep."

Karen let out a sob, her face dropping into my mother's neck. Mom patted her hair and eyed me, indicating it was my time to step up and speak.

I should have done what Alan did. I should have…

Too late now.

It was ten feet away but it felt like ten million. As Alan passed me to retake his seat, he pulled me in for a quick hug.

"Thank you," he said, his voice cracking.

Oh, God. Why?

I stepped behind the microphone. As I neared, it did that shrill, earsplitting shrieky sound thing. I winced and moved it farther away from my mouth. My hands trembled as I opened my notebook to the page with the words I'd crafted for the lifeless girl behind me.

"From the first day I met Quinn Littleton, I failed her."

I can't do this.

I sucked in a breath, my gaze lifting to my mother. She nodded at me encouragingly. Karen peered at me from between a few strands of Mom's dark hair, her handkerchief pressed to her mouth.

I have to do this.

Go, Emma. Go.

"From the first day I met Quinn Littleton, I failed her. I slept two doors down from her, in the same house. She occupied my spaces, she breathed my air, and yet I didn't know her. She liked cheerleading, and fashion, and makeup. She didn't like school but she did like photography. All of those facts you could find out from a stranger in a single five-minute conversation, yet it's all I can come up with when I talk about a girl I lived with.

"That's not Quinn's fault, it's mine, because from our first meeting, I judged her. I slapped a Mean Girl label on her and that was it. I didn't have to try anymore. In my head, Quinn was a cardboard cutout who existed not as an individual with hopes and dreams and fears, but as a purposeless wrecking ball. That's how I justified not giving her the respect she deserved. That's how I told myself it was okay to not bother being her friend or trying to understand her frustrations.

"I wish I'd gotten to know her better. I wish I'd not rejected her in favor of the unkind box I'd assigned her in my head. Everyone should get a chance, even the mean girl. Perhaps especially the mean girl, because she might have just needed someone to listen to her. I failed at that, and I hope, wherever Quinn is, she can forgive me for being so stupid. I might not deserve it, but I promise her that I've learned my lesson. Treat people with kindness even when kindness isn't the most obvious answer. Sometimes the hurts go deeper than anything we can see on the surface.

"Thank you."

I looked up at the crowd, at the hundreds of eyes pointed my way, some big, some small, some tearstained and some not. I looked at my boyfriend. I looked at my friends. I looked at my dad and the cheerleaders gathered to celebrate and mourn the girl behind me. There was no censure. No mockery. Where there could have been anger there were only people nodding along like maybe I'd said a smart thing. Like maybe it mattered.

I looked over at Karen. She sniffled and opened her arms to me, inviting me back to her and my mom and the family that remained. I closed my notebook and stepped down from the podium to take my seat. I examined Quinn's pale, perfect profile. It was partially my fault she was gone. I couldn't bring her back, but I could take her with me going forward. I could be nicer and less judgmental. I could give people a chance.

I could be a better person.

For that life lesson, I thanked Quinn Littleton.

And then, sandwiched between my moms, I finally cried for her.

* * * * *

ACKNOWLEDGMENTS

TO START: TO MY FRIENDS AND FAMILY. I LOVE YOU, I couldn't do this without you. Miriam Kriss? Rock star. Truly. Thank you for all you do. To the publishing team at Harlequin, more thanks. You are the frosting on my awesome cake. I'm proud of what we've made together. Evie Nelson, Becky Kroll—you edited this book not once, but twice, and I think you're amazing for it. Much love to you for being my second and third sets of eyes. One day we'll form a cool club and have T-shirts.

That said, *Dead Little Mean Girl* was a book born in frustration. I was watching TV, I can't even remember which show now and it really doesn't matter because it's such a prevalent trope, but on that show was the cardboard mean girl character lacking agency. She was mean for mean's sake. She ruined worlds because it was fun to ruin worlds. She was a sociopath because some lazy writer said she was.

It was frustrating, just like it's frustrating every single time I see this. The trope suggests some girls are just born mean. It suggests some girls take pleasure in damaging others. Rarely—never—is the reason for her cruelty examined because our society has determined that the humanity of this mean girl isn't important. Hating her for story's sake, however? Well, that's important.

For reasons. I guess.

As much as we loathe mustache-twirling villains in, say, a James Bond movie, or villains without logic or reason for their misdeeds in any book or film, why aren't we equally as enraged by the misogynistic portrayal of girls barely out of childhood? We're dismissing teenagers handily when there's a solid argument that in many of these cases, these girls are wearing their wounds on their sleeve. Something hurt them, they're angry and they respond with what they know best: more hurt. Yes, it's wrong what they do to others, and I'd never condone bullying of any kind. But it's also wrong to ignore girls screaming for help, and destroying as a practice is a pretty big flashing red light, don't you think?

Deep thoughts. I had them, and so a story germ was born.

Luckily, all of this coincided with my dear friend and now editor T.S. Ferguson asking me to write a dark comedy for him. *Dead Little Mean Girl*, then *Reputation*, was in concept much more *Heathers* meets *Mean Girls* in its conception. I loved it, as much as I love T.S., but when my words started pouring forth, what I got was far less funny than intended. We got a story with some snark, and some laughs, but a lot more feeling. Quinn was my complicated mean girl; she was the girl laying waste because something was desperately wrong with her. Emma, my protagonist, was the one on the sidelines, learning that Quinn wronged a lot of people, but no one stopping and asking how they could help Quinn was wrong in its fashion, too.

So this book is for T.S., who understood where I was going and why I went there, even though I produced something that wasn't exactly what he asked for. And it's for the girls who are dehumanized by the label of Mean Girl. And it's for the girls who have to survive Mean Girls, because I know they're out there, and I know the havoc they wreak, and I know how horrible it is for everyone. The teenaged girl is reviled in so many ways by our media. They're dismissed as silly, vacuous, self-involved, damaged. I'm tired of it, as all of us should be. This book is evidence of my fatigue, and a call for all of us to do better.

HJM